Y0-BTA-442

THE REEL THING

THE REEL THING

•

Beverly Martin-Lowry

&

Sue Blotz

AVALON BOOKS

NEW YORK

All the characters in this book are fictitious,
and any resemblance to actual persons,
living or dead, is purely coincidental.
Published by Thomas Bouregy & Co., Inc.
160 Madison Avenue, New York, NY 10016

Library of Congress Cataloging-in-Publication Data

Martin-Lowry, Beverly.
The reel thing / Beverly Martin-Lowry and Sue Blotz.
p. cm.
ISBN 0-8034-9783-0 (hardcover : acid-free paper)
I. Blotz, Sue. II. Title.

PS3613.A78628R44 2006
813'.6—dc22

2005037653

PRINTED IN THE UNITED STATES OF AMERICA
ON ACID-FREE PAPER
BY HADDON CRAFTSMEN, BLOOMSBURG, PENNSYLVANIA

Our deepest appreciation to Gil and Judy Dean,
whose invaluable firsthand knowledge and contribution
made a fleeting notion become a reality. Our heartfelt
thanks to you for the endless hours you contributed.
To our husbands and all our children, thank you
for your abiding patience and understanding
during our creative moments.

Chapter One

Megan's father had told her repeatedly to stay away from the movie crew that was filming in his south pasture. This economic boost was going to save the ranch, and he didn't want anything or anyone to spoil it. But, riding her horse through the early, cool morning air, accompanied by Bubba, her frisky mixed-breed dog, the young woman's curiosity kept growing and she decided to check out the surroundings.

Within ten minutes, she reached the far edge of the wooded area and stopped. Remaining silent and unnoticed in the shadow of trees, she watched a variety of activities taking place at the film crew's base camp, located in the middle of her dad's pasture.

The first thing she noticed was a man coming out of one of the ten or twelve travel trailers set up near the edge of the camp, each having its own generator for electricity. Beyond the trailers, she saw four men loading two trucks with plywood, large round posts, and bales of wire, material that she guessed would be used to build or add onto the movie set. Megan's attention was then turned to two women engaged in a heated conversation. The one wearing a costume similar in style to clothing worn in the nineteenth century—a long dress and starched bonnet—was pointing and shaking her finger at the other. *Yes*, Megan thought, *this is a busy place*.

It seemed strange having all this commotion going on where winter hay for the ranch animals was usually grown and where cows grazed after the harvesting was done. That wouldn't be happening in this pasture for a while.

Watching more people walk around the base camp—some fast, some slow—Megan guessed a few might be on their way to the large catering tent her dad had mentioned. Food was provided at all hours for the cast and crew.

Then, she looked toward the western edge of the camp and saw a tall, slim woman emerge from a parked semi-truck trailer, labeled MAKEUP. Even at this early hour, the actress was wearing a shimmering silver shirt, black jeans, and shin-high boots, obviously costumed for an early morning shoot. But it was the long, striking red hair, streaming loosely over her shoulders and down her back that caused recognition. Without a doubt, this was Angela Taylor, star of *Running Bull*, the movie being filmed on her dad's large, central Texas ranch.

The actress walked over and got into a chauffeur-driven vehicle. She probably was going to the main set, a newly built, prefabricated western town, located to the rear of Megan's father's property, where most of the filming was being shot.

During recent years, quite a few movies, some receiving rave reviews and awards, had been made in Austin, Texas and neighboring counties, which had now been dubbed Little Hollywood. Famous celebrities had taken up permanent residence in the area, building large, elegant homes. All of this, of course, provided excitement and interest for the local population. Also, dollars being spent in the process had gone a long way to stimulate the area's economy and had even increased a number of personal bank accounts. Megan's dad was hoping to join this fortunate group.

Several months earlier, Oliver Plum's movie company had sent scouts out to research Jim Wakefield's ranch as a possible location on which to film *Running Bull*. Twice before, Wakefield's place had been surveyed, but then was turned down because it didn't have the terrain needed for a certain story plot.

This third time was the charm, however, and within days after the contract was signed, crews arrived to begin construction of an old western town on his property. Just the fronts of wooden buildings were erected, painted to give the impression of being authentic, and placed on both sides of the newly created, one-block, Western-style main street. A real structure, designed in the same manner, but containing walled rooms and a roof, was built, as well. It housed several indoor sets; a saloon, an office, a bedroom, and more. These rooms were decorated and outfitted to provide proper background for different scenes in the script.

At the same time, an area called base camp was created and that's what Megan was now looking at. Tents, RVs, temporary buildings and semi-trailers were brought in; even an animal corral was constructed. When all of this was in place, the stars, director, and producers arrived and filming began.

This cattle ranch had been in the Wakefield family for decades. Like Megan, her dad had grown up here with the ranch being his entire life and only source of income. And then, fifteen years ago, Jim's widowed father was killed in a tractor accident and her dad became sole owner.

But recently, due to several seasons of drought, Jim had been forced to sell off a fourth of his cattle herd in order to remain financially solvent. And, as her dad had told Megan, he really didn't know what would have happened if this film company and their weekly checks hadn't come along when they did. Now, and for as long as it took to make this movie, Wakefield would be able to provide food for his family, feed for the animals, pay bills, and maybe even have enough money left over for some long-needed extras. He still prayed for rain, however, and lots of it, even though, for obvious reasons, the film company preferred that it stay dry.

Megan saw a chauffeured van pull up in front of the catering tent and its passenger, a man who looked familiar, got out. *Who is that guy?* She was sure that he was a well-known actor, someone whose movie she had seen recently, but couldn't put a name with the face.

And, that's when Megan got the insane idea to go over and casually intermingle with others there at the camp. Though the thought was frightening, it excited her. *No one will know if I belong here or not. Why, I can even stroll into the food tent and talk to some of the people; maybe even strike up a conversation with that guy who just arrived.* But, she couldn't do this on horseback as that would attract far too much attention.

So, getting down from the saddle, she led her mare over to a nearby tree and wrapped the lead rope around a lower limb. Giving the animal's nose a quick pat, Megan set off to the camp. But, Bubba, who earlier had wandered a short distance back into the trees, probably to check out some interesting smell, looked up just then, and saw he was being left behind. The dog began to run after his mistress, barking loudly, which caused the horse to rear up, breaking loose from the tree. Soon, both animals were charging full force, across the pasture and toward the movie's base of operations.

Megan had just reached the camp when the commotion erupted. Now, looking over at the truck being loaded with wood, she saw one of the young men jump aside just in time to avoid being hit by the runaway horse, which was headed in her direction.

Oh my goodness, what have I done? Instinctively, she ran toward her mare, but the animal dodged her attempt to grab the reins. Then, the horse turned and headed straight for the catering tent. Though running as fast as she could, Megan realized there was no way she could prevent this pending disaster.

Then, just as her horse ran by the row of parked RVs, a young man came out from behind one of them and, with unusual agility and quickness, managed to grab the reins. Using the weight from his body, as he was pulled along, the man finally brought the mare to a stop, just inches before it plowed into the huge food tent.

Several people who were watching all this action-packed, though unfilmed chaos, witnessed Megan running breathlessly over to the man holding onto her mare.

"Is this your horse?" he demanded.

"Yes, and thanks for catching her," Megan answered, still winded from the run. Her interest quickly switched from her horse to the man as she watched him push an untamed lock of dark, almost black hair from his forehead. That done, the six-foot, lean but muscular guy turned and focused warm, brown eyes directly on Megan, causing her pulse rate to accelerate.

She guessed him to be close to her age, early to mid-twenties, and he seemed quite comfortable around large animals. However, as he continued to hold the reins and rub the horse's nose, Megan grew anxious. So, extending her hand, she said, "I'll take her, now."

But, instead of handing over the leather straps, he pulled them even further from her grasp. "You beginners shouldn't be allowed to run free with horses or any other large animals. You don't have a clue as to how much harm you can do."

"Beginner? Run free? Clue?" gasped Megan. "I'll have you know I'm not a beginner. I've been riding most of my life."

"Oh, yeah, I can really see that." His voice was full of sarcasm. "But, lady, I'm serious. Be careful. Here, take the reins and go back to wherever it is you came from. And please keep that horse away from this area. If I hadn't been here just now to catch her, we could have had a major disaster."

Thoroughly embarrassed, and without another word, Megan claimed her mare and began walking with the animal, away from the camp. After going only a short distance, she turned and glared at the young man who was still watching her. So, in a show of defiance, Megan climbed up into the saddle and, with a loud "Yeehaw," galloped off toward the woods. Imagining what he must be thinking at that moment, or even saying, Megan began to laugh and all her embarrassment vanished.

Gil Sanders had found that being calm and attentive was a necessity when dealing with animals, especially those bigger him. Controlling them physically was difficult and, unless proper care was taken, it could become disastrous. Gil constantly worked to keep his emotions in check and tried to use his brain, instead. But, what really made him angry was human stupidity, a category he applied to the girl and her horse.

Soon, however, his annoyance switched over to anger at himself. Having caught the horse, he knew he should have read her the riot act about letting the animal get away. But all he could think of, right then, was how young and pretty she looked; how her scarlet lipstick emphasized the whiteness of her teeth, and that her slim, five-foot-four, well-shaped body seemed to be catching the attention of all the guys in the area. Of course, there was that blond hair, cut short and spiked. Usually, Gil preferred long, flowing tresses but he had to admit, she looked cute and the style suited her well.

"Hey, Gil, nice going, boy!" one of the men called out, jolting him back to the present. "Don't know what would have happened if you hadn't stopped that horse when you did."

"Thanks, Ted, but it was just luck and being in the right place at the right time. When I came around the corner on my way to wardrobe and saw that wild thing coming right at me, those automatic reflexes kicked in. Oh man! Speaking of wardrobe, I'd better get over there, now. I'm due on the set shortly." So, with that, Gil took off running toward one of the five semi-trailers.

Each trailer was equipped to handle a specific need.

One held makeup supplies plus well-lit, mirrored tables where the cast members sat as professionals applied the necessary touches.

Costumes and apparel were stored in another trailer, which also contained dressing rooms, a washer, dryer, and ironing board. Props, however, were housed in a separate unit.

Also, there was 'The Honey Wagon.' This trailer provided temporary comfort for the performing stars and other important members of the crew. At night, or when not working, this group stayed elsewhere, usually at some choice hotel or nearby motel. But, when on the set and needing temporary quarters, they used The Honey Wagon's deluxe private rest areas and bathrooms.

At the wardrobe trailer, Gil was handed chaps, vest, and a wide-brimmed cowboy hat so he could pose as the stuntman doubling for Wade Dillon, the movie's male star. Having arrived in jeans, denim shirt, and boots, he was able to add these new items quickly. Next, after spending some time in makeup, Gil went on to the prop trailer and picked up a saddle, holster, and rubber gun. Should the story line require actual shooting, usually done with blanks, a prop man would bring a real gun to the set, loaded and ready to use.

Gil loved this work. The problem was it lasted only, at the most, a few months, maybe only a few weeks, and sometimes was canceled before it even started. But Gil found it to be an exciting and stimulating way to make a buck. And, it sure beat the jobs he took on to support himself between movie gigs, like cowboy and ranch work.

As he walked across the camp on his way to the corral, tempting aromas wafted out from the catering tent. However, that morning's episode with the runaway horse had eliminated his chance to eat, so he had to put his growling stomach on hold.

Geronimo, his horse and four-legged friend, was waiting for Gil and, seeing him approach, trotted over to the corral fence and began to snort and toss his head. After a quick pat on the nose and using some sugar cubes as bait, Gil encouraged Geronimo to follow him to the far side of the pen to be saddled. Already, bright sun was beginning to warm the air. The TV weatherman had promised mid-seventies temperatures, making this day just about perfect for the work Gil was scheduled to do.

Leading Geronimo out of the corral, he closed and secured the gate before climbing up into the saddle. Soon, they were galloping across a large open pasture toward the movie set; both thoroughly enjoying this wild sense of freedom.

Gil mentally crossed his fingers, hoping Paul Eller, the director, would start filming his stunt on time. But, having been through this before, he knew the probability of that happening was slim to none and they would, no doubt, be running at least two hours late.

So, with this in mind, Gil slowed down his horse to a

walk and that's when he saw two men with cameras, shooting pictures of moving cattle, probably to use as a fill-in scene. The men were up high in buckets, known as condors, driven by hydraulic lifts. This allowed the men to stay out of the way while they approached and filmed from various angles. During evening or night shots, these mechanical devices were also used to carry and move around powerful lights.

Then, out of nowhere, Gil's mind asked once again, just who was that girl with the horse? Movie locations were supposed to be secured and the people employed were required to wear name tags. But, of course, suppliers not directly connected to film-making, like UPS, FedEx, Graham Food Company and others were allowed to come and go without much difficulty. This girl, however, was definitely not one of them.

Since becoming involved with the film industry, Gil had come into contact with quite a few glamorous and gorgeous women; so why was this one, though attractive—even sexy—still in his mind and nagging at him? Like it or not, he was interested and would make it a point to find out exactly who she was and why she was there. Her spirited attitude had irritated him at first, but now he couldn't help but smile at the thought of her.

It was almost nine o'clock when Megan and her horse, on their way home, emerged from the woods. After passing the fenced-in pastures and several corrals, Megan finally reached a large barn where she dismounted and unsaddled the animal. After giving it a good brushing, she took the horse back outside, put it in one of the corrals, and watched as it ran over to the water trough.

Then Megan walked the short distance over to her parents' house. Actually, it was her house, too, though for the last four years she had lived in Lubbock while attending Texas Tech.

But when Megan reached the patio, she panicked. How could she ever explain to her parents the fiasco at the movie's base camp? After all, she wasn't even supposed to be there—had been told emphatically by her father to keep her distance. But maybe, if she didn't say anything, they'd never find out and it would all be forgotten. Then again, with the way news traveled around town, that probably wasn't going to happen.

And, just who was that guy anyway, the one who had caught her horse? This question had bothered her during the ride home. She didn't recognize him as being an actor in any movie she'd ever seen. However, many people appear in shows and movies with bit parts and aren't remembered from one film to the next. But, surely, she would have remembered this one. Not only was he a hunk, but he also seemed to have a way with animals. She really wouldn't mind running into him again sometime, though hopefully under circumstances that didn't make her look like such a fool.

Walking across the patio and through the back door, Megan found her mom in the kitchen, putting dough into the bread machine. While away at school, she had really missed her mother's cooking. Sure, the meals they served in the cafeteria were okay—well, most of the time—and there were plenty of fast-food restaurants in the Lubbock area, but it just wasn't the same.

"Did you have a good ride?" her mother, Naomi, asked with interest.

"Sure did, Mom. Yes, I sure did. Riding is something I really missed while I was away at school."

"Well, now that you've graduated and have your degree in business, what are you going to do next? I realize you wanted to take the summer off to catch your breath, but it's time you decided on a course of action and plan for the future." Megan knew where her mother was going with all this, but she didn't want to talk about it now or maybe ever. Unlike her mom, the girl was not an organizer. She didn't even like to think that way. Megan would rather coast along and see what happened; let nature take its course. But, her mother wasn't going to allow this. She would keep insisting her daughter come up with a plan.

"I haven't thought much about it yet, but I will soon, I promise."

"Why don't you go look at the want ads in today's newspaper for starters?" Megan could tell that her mom wasn't going to give up. "Maybe you can find something interesting and then begin sending out resumes. You know, something to get the ball rolling."

"I'll do that, Mom, but first I need to take a shower and change my clothes. I smell like a horse."

"Oh, didn't Dad tell you? He needs your help this morning, so you probably should wait a bit before taking that shower. He wants you to help him look for several cows that broke through the fence last night down by the river."

Just then, her father, a man in his late forties, entered the kitchen wearing a denim shirt with the collar unbuttoned, faded blue jeans, and heavy work boots. "Oh there you are, girl! Mom said you went out for an early ride. Everything go okay?"

"Sure, Dad, everything was fine." *Liar, liar, pants on fire*, Megan thought, realizing she had just gone with the don't-ask-don't-tell option.

"Well, did Mom mention I need your help this morning?"

"Yes, she was just telling me that." Megan really didn't mind helping her dad. In fact, she'd much rather do that than spend time looking for an office job. But, the question, *Why did I just waste four years in college getting a degree in business*? ran through her mind. And the answer, *Because that's what Dad wanted me to do*, followed it.

Chapter Two

As Gil earlier feared, most of the day disappeared before they even began shooting his part in the film. After they finally did start, all went well and he was quite satisfied with both his and Geronimo's performance. Even Paul Eller, the director, seemed pleased and almost nothing ever satisfied him.

When Eller yelled, "That's a wrap," Gil looked up and to his surprise, saw Angela Taylor, the movie's female lead, standing off to one side of the set. The actress seemed to be watching him intently, which was odd. And, when she realized that he had seen and recognized her, the actress smiled and waved at Gil before turning to leave, making the moment even more strange. Angela rarely wasted her valuable time observing the actions or acting abilities of lesser cast members.

It took another fifteen minutes or so before Gil was officially dismissed for the day. But, holding onto the reins of his horse, he finally started down the dirt street of the simulated western town and out toward the real world. Not paying much attention to the activity of those around him, he reached the end of the set and that's when Gil saw her again. This time Angela was leaning casually against her chauffeured vehicle in front of him.

"Hey," the actress called out. "It's Gil, isn't it?"

"Yes?" Now, though somewhat flattered, he was really baffled. Why was this beautiful starlet, with her large violet eyes and long, flowing red hair, making such an effort to approach him? It made no sense, nor did her explanation.

"I wanted to tell you, Gil, that I was so impressed with the way you handled yourself and your horse. Having him fall like that, on your command, was incredible. And then, the way you fell off, too, making it look so real, but not even hurting yourself; now, that was impressive!"

Gil found himself speechless. Usually the stars in a movie, although polite and sometimes friendly, didn't socialize or associate much off-stage with lesser actors or employees. But, here was this famous woman making it a point to personally meet with him, and all he could do was wonder why. However, he did manage a, "Thank you, Angela. It's nice of you to say so."

"No problem, Gil," and she continued to stand there leaving Gil unsure of what to do or say next.

It was Angela who finally broke the silence. "Say, maybe we could meet in town later and grab a bite to eat, my treat." The very attractive woman five or six years older than his twenty-five years looked up at him and smiled. As she moved closer, her pose alluring and dramatic, Gil detected the light scent of gardenia.

It almost seemed as if she was coming on to him. And, though thrilled by the attention, Gil didn't know what to say. He found Angela to be beautiful but also way out of his league economically, socially, and professionally. So finally he came up with, "Yeah, I'd like that, but can't make it tonight. I've already got plans. Maybe some other time we can."

Her smile took on new depth and she gave Gil her full attention. But whether this was real or just good acting, he didn't know. Then, after maintaining this facial expression and quiet stare for several more seconds, Angela's attitude began to grow more intimidating. "Okay Gil, then how about tomorrow night?"

He realized she wasn't about to give up and having no more excuses on hand, Gil politely agreed. He was told to meet her at seven o'clock the following evening at The Pines, one of the nicer and more expensive restaurants in downtown Wayside. With a final wave and a subtle sway of her hips, Angela walked back to her van while a flabbergasted Gil and his horse just stood there.

Gil hadn't a clue as to why he had hesitated so long before accepting her offer. Most guys would have given anything to date such a gorgeous and famous woman. And, maybe that was exactly his reason. With all her choices, why did she pick him? Something didn't seem right. Or, he was being foolish and she actually was attracted to him.

As her car drove off, and while swinging up into the saddle, Gil thought he saw movement over at a fake doorway on the set. Looking more closely, he recognized Eller standing there. However, before Gil could speak or even acknowledge the director, he turned abruptly and walked in the opposite direction, his attitude clearly one of controlled anger. *What's that all about*? Gil wondered.

He knew only a little about Eller's background. The man, in his mid-forties, had been a part of the movie industry for most of his life. He played bit parts as a teenager, having a few lines in several movies. Entering his twenties, he was given larger roles. But Eller's first love and primary interest had always been directing. Finally, at the young age of thirty, he was offered a director's position on a low budget film. And, to everyone's surprise, it became an enormous success. It was due to this that Eller's career took off. Offers to direct other movies, more than he could ever accept, began pouring in. So why, Gil wondered, would such a savvy and successful person like Eller hide in the shadows and watch a conversation between the star of his film and a stuntman?

Gil, now in open pasture, prodded his horse to a full gallop. Both he and the animal seemed to need, at that moment, the thrill of moving swiftly and the feel of fresh wind. It was a natural high and one he took pleasure in. Then, although still some distance from base camp, Gil slowed the horse down so he could enjoy the peace and quiet while ambling along after a very busy day.

Even though he hadn't grown up on a ranch, Gil had, as a boy, been blessed by meeting someone who did own one; someone who had taken the time to teach him not only how to ride a horse, but also how to care for a variety of animals. This helped Gil to decide to pursue these interests after graduating from high school.

In time, this love for animals led to his involvement with the movie industry. One encounter with the film world was all Gil needed, to know that he wanted to be a permanent part of this business and make it his primary means of support. So far, though, his involvement had been limited, but it was growing.

And that's why seeing Eller walk away in obvious anger was worrisome. Only ten or fifteen minutes earlier, the two men had stood at the corral, shaking hands and bidding each other a friendly good-bye. The director, though usually tense due to the stress of his job, had been, at that moment, calm and serene and had even complimented Gil on his performance. The first take had gone perfectly, though they did do another one as backup. And, in the movie business, things don't get much better than that.

His thoughts turned, then, to Angela and her invitation for dinner. What brought that on? Although she was famous and not lacking in good looks, she really wasn't his type nor, Gil guessed, was he hers. So, why was she coming on to him? And, while it didn't make any sense, he certainly didn't want to offend her. But maybe if they did get better acquainted, she would put in a good word here and there, causing more offers for jobs to come his way. A lot of movie employment occurred because someone higher up in the business vouched for someone else.

While Gil enjoyed being a stunt man, he also liked being head wrangler, supplying and caring for the animals used in movies and commercials. This not only created an increase in his paycheck, but helped the young man add more animals to his personal collection, currently being kept on a friend's nearby ranch.

Also, there was his secret desire to work as an actor. So maybe, just maybe, if Angela was willing to spread the word about his talents to the right people, who knew what might happen? But there was no way Gil would have a romantic relationship with her or anyone else just to promote his career, even though in the movie industry this did happen.

When the actress extended her dinner invitation, Gil actually had no plans for that evening but his spontaneous response just popped out and he was glad it had. Now, he had more than twenty-four hours to get his thinking straight and figure out how to handle it gracefully and maybe to his own advantage.

Gil and Geronimo continued to wander along slowly until the base camp, still off in the distance, came into view. Another busy day was ending there. People were milling about, trying to wrap things up and Gil realized he wasn't feeling very social or in the mood for small talk, something that would be expected when reaching camp. So, pulling hard on the reins, he turned Geronimo around and headed in a different direction. Not back the way he had come but instead, westward, toward the river. He was still on the Wakefield ranch, just not in an area the movie company had contracted for use.

The breeze that tickled the leaves all day had become quiet, leaving the atmosphere pleasant for Gil and Geronimo as they made their way through the native wild grass. The afternoon sun was slowly edging down toward the horizon though they still had an hour or so before the sky would turn dark.

Leaving the pasture, the horse began weaving its way through underbrush and trees. Gil noticed the animal's ears perk up and before long he, too, began hearing strange sounds he couldn't identify. However, upon reaching a ledge overlooking the river bank, he discovered the answer. The noise was a mixture of water splashing, cow mooing, dog growling, and a female voice calling out.

Gil was amazed to see, out in the river, the same girl who had started his day off with such unexpected and abrasive excitement. Now, here she was again, but this time, trying to catch a cow instead of a horse. At the moment, both were knee deep in a shallow portion of river. The girl, with a rope around the cow's neck, was pulling firmly, trying to convince it to come back on shore. Meanwhile, a dog kept running noisily along the river's edge, changing its tone from harsh barks to low growls.

As Gil watched, he saw the girl again pull tightly on the rope. This time, as she stepped backward, she slipped and fell while the cow tried to escape. In spite of it all, she held on but couldn't seem to regain her footing and the animal slowly began pulling her into deeper water.

Gil realized he had to do something and do it fast. Jumping down from his horse, he threw the reins over a tree limb. Then, sliding his way down the embankment, Gil ran as fast as he could over to the river where he shed his vest, chaps, hat, and boots before jumping in.

Luckily, the current wasn't very strong and he managed to reach the girl quickly. By now the water was almost to his waist and to her shoulders. While the girl held onto the rope attached to the cow, Gil grabbed her around the waist and managed to get her back to her feet. And, though the cow could no longer reach the river's bottom, it managed to stay afloat.

Gil discovered that just holding onto this girl was becoming dangerous. Her body, now pressed against his, was causing him to drown, not in the river's moving current, but in the subtle fragrance arising from her hair and skin. Then, she turned her head and a full crimson mouth was lifted toward him, unconsciously seductive and sensuous. Though she said nothing, Gil believed the girl was aware of his tension, and could see in his eyes evidence of the heat and passion rapidly growing inside him.

Still in control of himself, Gil carefully let go of the girl's waist and, taking her hand, began to pull her back toward shore. She hung onto the rope and brought the cow along as well. It took several minutes, but finally the three were on dry land. Neither Gil nor the girl said anything though her dog seemed pleased and continued to bark loudly. Even the cow bellowed a few loud moos.

Trying to catch her breath, the girl stood there in a soaked navy turtleneck shirt and blue jeans. She seemed totally unaware that the effect was both sexy and seductive. When finally able to speak, she asked, "What are you doing here?"

"I guess I'm pulling you out of the river," was his sharp retort. Soaking wet and no longer holding hands, both began to feel the evening chill. The sun, by now, was almost over the horizon and the air was cooling off rapidly. So, fighting off the urge to once again gather her up into his arms, Gil asked, "Why are you still here on the ranch and what were you doing out in that river, anyway?"

Brushing the short, wet, blond hair from her forehead, she answered indignantly, "What am I doing here? I happen to live on this ranch and I was trying to rescue a cow. I chased this cow while my dad went after two others over there, on the far side of that fence. But, before I could catch up to this brainless beast, it ran into the river. I tried, first, to coax it out, but finally had to go in after her. At least I did manage to get the rope around her neck and that helped." Gil noticed, then, that the girl was shivering.

"Well, we're going to have to get you home right away before you catch pneumonia. Where's your truck or your horse? How did you get down here? Did you come on foot?" Gil knew he was rambling and asking too many questions all at once.

"My dad and I rode horses, but we left them tied up, way over in the other pasture. Since I haven't returned, I'm sure Dad will take mine home with him and check to see if I've made it okay. He knows it's closer and easier for me to walk to the house from here than to try and go back and get my horse."

"Well, mine's right here so you can ride with me, but first we have to get up that incline. Tell you what; you hold onto the cow while I climb up there. Then, I'll reach over the edge and help pull you both up."

Much to his own amazement, Gil's plan went smoothly. He had Megan sit behind him in the saddle, a snug fit, but he didn't mind. Reaching out, he took her arm and pulled it around his waist for safety, while her other hand held onto the rope still attached to the cow's neck. Bubba, the dog, no longer barking, was running a short distance ahead.

Though wet and cold, Gil enjoyed the feel of her closeness. He realized, now, that this girl was no shrinking violet but a prime twenty-two or twenty-three-year-old in full bloom who was strong and yet very feminine. She seemed, however, totally unaware of her attractiveness.

Twenty minutes later they reached her house and although Gil was growing colder by the minute, for him the trip ended much too soon. Their timing was perfect, however, as they found Jim Wakefield in his pickup, about to go back down to the river in search of his daughter.

Because the veil of evening darkness was beginning to settle in, Wakefield hadn't seen them until they were almost to the house. When he did catch sight of the strange group headed his way, Wakefield jumped out of his truck and ran toward them, wanting to know what had happened. Gil asked him to please wait for the details until they got the cow into a pen and his daughter inside the house and Wakefield agreed. With both of them working together, they got the job done quickly and before long, Gil, after leaving his muddy, wet boots out on the patio, entered the warm, cozy kitchen.

Jim asked Gil to follow him into the living room where Naomi Wakefield was waiting. Megan, however, headed down the hallway, in the opposite direction, and

Gil guessed she was about to exchange her wet clothes for some dry ones. Because of his own damp condition, the young man refused the chair Naomi offered, but instead stood there and introduced himself to the older couple. After first clarifying that he was part of the movie company, Gil went on to explain why he happened to be at the river, and what took place.

Naomi, who seemed to be watching him intently, finally spoke up. "You need some dry clothes or you're going to catch your death of cold, if you haven't already. I think Jim has a sweat suit that might fit, one you can use until you get back to your place and your own things. Let me go check." Naomi hurried from the room and neither man spoke until she returned with a dark green top and matching pants which she handed over to Gil.

"You can use the bathroom there at the end of the hall to change into these. And, here's a plastic sack for you to put your wet clothes in."

After a quick thank you, Gil made his way down the hallway and into the empty bathroom. He was feeling quite cold and didn't waste any time changing. So it wasn't long before he found himself back in the living room, now dry and holding a sack of wet clothes. The Wakefield couple, however, had disappeared. Instead, the girl he had just rescued from the river was sitting on the couch, also freshly attired.

"I'm sorry. I don't even know your name," he said.

"Well, since we keep running into each other, I guess

maybe we should introduce ourselves. My name is Megan, Megan Wakefield. And yours?"

"Gil Sanders. I'm a stunt man in the movie. I'm also head wrangler and supply any animals they might need."

"Well, that helps explain how you managed to grab my horse so quickly this morning, you being an expert and all."

"I don't know about the expert part, but I happened to be in the right place at the right time." Gil began to feel uncomfortable. He wasn't coming across as well as he wanted to. *Why am I trying to impress her?* So far, the girl had been nothing but a disaster waiting to happen. Though, in all honesty, he really didn't mind.

Gil noticed that Megan seemed nervous as well, and even though he didn't want to, decided maybe he should leave. Instead, though, he invited her out for a bite to eat that evening, surprising both himself and the girl. Without hesitation, Megan smiled and accepted. Another shock for Gil as she actually seemed pleased, maybe even a little excited.

"Since it's close to six o'clock, how about I pick you up around eight and this time I'll bring my truck, not a horse?"

Megan, rising from the couch, agreed and then walked with him into the kitchen where they found her parents at the table, drinking coffee. Naomi offered Gil a cup, which he declined, explaining that he needed to get back to his RV and get cleaned up.

Jim Wakefield got to his feet and, shaking Gil's hand,

said, "Thanks so much for all your help. If there's ever anything we can do for you, don't hesitate to ask. We owe you one."

"No problem, sir. I'm just glad I was there to lend a hand. But now, I'd better get going so I can be back in time to pick up your daughter. We're going out for dinner, if that's all right with you both." Gil looked over and saw Naomi smile and nod her head in approval. She actually seemed pleased. And Gil was relieved to see that by his relaxed demeanor Wakefield, too, was okay with his daughter's dinner plans. In fact, he even walked Gil out to the corral and watched while he mounted the horse. Gil, anxious for the evening to begin, waved a quick good-bye and hurried back to camp.

Wakefield's ranch was about fifteen miles outside the town of Wayside and Megan, who had lived there her entire life, suggested Toby's, a combination bar and café known for its excellent down-home cooking. Both chose and enjoyed steak, hash browns, and a salad, topped it off with a slice of pecan pie for dessert.

Conversation was a little stilted at first until Megan got Gil to open up and talk about himself. That's when she learned he had grown up an only child in a small West Texas town. "Dad died when I was ten," Gil explained, "and my mother raised me while working as a waitress to support us."

"That must have been hard for her."

"It was, but the owner of the café where she worked

seemed to like me and so did his wife. They owned a small ranch at the edge of town, within walking distance from both my house and school so they invited me to stop by any time I wanted."

"That was nice."

"Yes, it was. In fact, before long, I was spending most of my free time there after school and all day during the summers, helping the owner's wife, Beth, do ranch chores. That's how I got acquainted with animals and learned so much about them.

"Then one day Beth offered to teach me how to ride a horse. I was so excited. It took a few weeks, but before long I was very comfortable and in control. When she saw this, Beth let me ride alone on the ranch as often as I wanted."

"So why did you and your mom move?" Megan's curiosity was growing.

"That's because her boss died when I was a sophomore in high school. Beth had to close down the café and since the town was small, no other job openings were available. So, Mom moved us to Austin where she found work right away. Then, she met George, a truck driver. He used to stop in regularly at the restaurant where she was a waitress and after dating for a year or so, they got married."

"And you like this man, your stepfather?"

"Well . . ."

"Come on, you can say, do you like him?" Megan was insistent.

Gil didn't seem to know quite how to respond. "I guess I like George. He's a kind and generous man, but at that point in my life I resented having to share my mom with anyone. So I didn't spend much time at home. During that first summer I cut grass and earned enough money to buy an old pickup. Then, the week after I graduated from high school, I packed up what few belongings I had and moved from the city.

"Since I wanted to be on my own, away from my mom and George, I went to nearby ranches and found part-time work as a wrangler and livestock caretaker. Then, after a year, I saved up enough money to buy a newer pickup plus a used RV. This helped out a lot. I could keep my stuff inside the mobile home and didn't have to camp outside or sleep in other people's barns.

"When I turned twenty-one, I moved to a ranch near Bastrop to work and became close friends with the owner's son, Gary, who was my age. We not only enjoyed working together as a team on the ranch, but also spent our off-hours together, having fun in town. One day, when we were bored and didn't have anything to do, we started to train a young dog there on the ranch and eventually were able to get it to act on command and do tricks."

"Wow! You guys did that?" Megan was impressed.

"Yep, in fact, it went so well we began surfing the Internet to get information on how to train horses. Gary had a young mare on the ranch so we began there and it worked. After that, we trained several more horses and, before long, had about five skilled to some degree. We also worked with a big pig and a couple of goats.

"Then, one night, while we were hanging out at a popular club in Bastrop, a guy connected with the movie business struck up a conversation. He happened to mention that the commercial he was involved with was looking for a trained pig to film. Well, Gary and I both spoke at once, telling him we had one. And, that's how my movie career got started.

"It took time but eventually we were receiving more and more requests to provide animals for commercials and movies in the area. Then, a movie company called, asking if we had a trained mule. It just so happened we did and, before long, our efforts began to pay off even more."

"But, where's Gary now?" Megan was really getting into this.

"Gary decided he was more interested in the business side of things while I liked the physical part, the actual training and animal care. Consequently, Gary now works for a promotion company in Austin, while I still try to earn a living training and supplying animals. We've remained good friends, though."

"Where do you keep these animals?"

"I keep them on Gary's dad's ranch. He lets them stay there, free of charge, in exchange for my help when he needs it. I have a good animal collection right now and was even able to buy Geronimo, who's well-trained as a fall horse. He's brought in even more job offers."

Megan was impressed, though Gil, realizing he'd just poured out his whole life's story, seemed embarrassed. Actually, Megan had found it fascinating and was pleased that he had been comfortable enough to share all this with her. So, in exchange, she decided to admit her own secret desire.

"My dad wants me to get a corporate job in some big company and work my way up. Because of that, my major in college was business. But, during the summer months at Tech, I took classes in animal science and received a secondary degree as a veterinary technician. Dad knew I was doing this; he even paid for my classes, but figured it was merely a hobby. I, on the other hand, really want this to be my profession but, so far, I haven't been able to tell him that. Dad lives back in the dark ages and believes women, if they have to, should work in offices."

Megan noticed that her story captured Gil's interest too. At first, he seemed surprised, but then pleased. However, just as he was about to make a comment, his attention was caught by someone entering the café. This person also appeared to recognize Gil, and after a moment's pause, walked over to the table.

"Well, it seems you have a busy life, Gil," the man said. Then, looking at Megan, he held out his hand. "Hi. My name's Paul Eller."

Gil quickly stood up, preparing to introduce her. Though not understanding why, Megan could feel tension between the two men. "Paul, this is Megan Wakefield. Her father owns the ranch where we're filming. And, Megan, this is Paul Eller, our director."

After shaking her hand, Megan was surprised when Eller continued holding onto it in a possessive sort of way. "My dear, have you ever done any acting?" he asked.

"Me? No, I haven't. This is the closest I've ever been to the movie industry."

"Well, you need to drop in and watch us sometime. Feel free to come by whenever you like. I'll leave your name with security and you can come and go without a problem."

"Thank you, Mr. Eller," she said. "I'd love to do that."

"Please, call me Paul."

Gil spoke up. "Megan's already dropped in on us. Just this morning, she and her horse came by the camp to pay us a surprise visit."

"Oh?" said Eller. "I didn't know that and I don't remember seeing you."

Gil went on to explain, "You were probably on the set and missed all the excitement."

Megan, by this time, was very uncomfortable and she couldn't imagine why Gil had brought all this up. Was it to embarrass her? She thought the whole episode had been put to rest, but now, here he was, bringing it up again.

Attempting to change the subject, Megan said, "I was just telling Gil that I minored in veterinary science in college."

"You did?" Eller asked with piqued interest.

Megan continued, "I can't do all that a vet does, but I'm very knowledgeable and would be happy to help out, if needed."

She saw a look of disapproval cross Gil's face. Surely he didn't think she was invading his turf?

But Eller thanked Megan for her offer and said he just might take her up on it. And, after politely declining Gil's invitation to join them, he crossed the room to sit at another table, alone. Several times, Megan caught him staring over at them and wondered what that was all about.

Eller's arrival changed the evening's previously pleasant atmosphere and now neither Gil nor Megan seemed to find anything to say so they just ate their dessert in silence. Gil, after finishing, said that since he had an early schedule the next day, maybe they should head back to the ranch. Megan quickly agreed.

Later though, as Gil escorted her to the front door of her house, and after she thanked him for dinner, Megan didn't know if she was glad or disappointed that he didn't ask to see her again. As to how she felt about the absence of a goodnight kiss, well, she made a point of not letting her thoughts even go there.

Chapter Three

The following morning, when she opened her eyes, Megan found her mother standing at the bedroom door. "You have a phone call."

"A phone call?" She was still half asleep. "Who's calling me at this hour?" It was only six o'clock.

"I don't know, but you might want to get up and talk to him. It's some man whose voice I don't recognize."

Grabbing a robe and putting on slippers, Megan followed her mother down the hallway and into the kitchen where she picked up the wall phone.

"Hello?"

"Hi, Megan, this is Paul Eller. We met last night, remember?"

"Oh, yes, Mr. Eller. I remember."

"I think I asked you to call me Paul," the man said laughing.

"Yes, you did, Paul, I'm sorry. Can I help you?" Megan was curious why he would be calling her, especially at this hour.

"I believe last night you mentioned something about having been trained as a veterinary technician. Is that correct?"

"Yes, I did. Why? Do you need some help with your animals?"

"Well, yes, I do. If you can, I need you to look at a goat. He's scheduled to appear in a scene this afternoon, but he doesn't seem right. If necessary, I'll call a vet, but first, I thought maybe you could check him over."

"What seems to be the problem, Paul?"

"Instead of going into all of this over the phone, could you just come and meet me here as soon as possible?"

"Where are you? I'm not all that familiar with your setup."

"Oh, I'm at the base camp and I won't be leaving for at least another hour. Do you think you can get here before then?"

"Yes, I'm sure I can."

"Okay. I'll see you soon."

Megan hung up and found both her mother and father standing in the kitchen, staring at her.

"What was that all about?" her father asked.

"It was Paul Eller, the director of the movie. I met him last night at the café while Gil and I were having dinner. Somehow it came up in the conversation that I have a degree as a vet tech and he has a goat that he's worried about."

Her mom and dad exchanged a strange look, one that Megan chose to ignore. Instead, she hurried back to her room where she exchanged her pajamas for jeans and a T-shirt. Making a quick pass through the bathroom, she brushed her teeth, ran a comb through her short, spiky blond hair, and applied some lipstick. Then, back in the kitchen, and after saying good-bye to her parents and Bubba, Megan grabbed her boots off the newspaper on the floor by the back door, slipped them on, and ran out to the corral. It took several minutes to get her horse saddled, but soon Megan was mounted and making her way through the wooded area.

She wondered what her parents were thinking at the moment, especially since all this was certainly confusing even to her. Though pleased that he had called, she questioned why Eller hadn't asked Gil to look at the goat, which was his job. But, since Megan was still upset that Gil had mentioned her horse incident to the director at dinner the previous evening, she felt this just might make things even.

As for her parents, Megan knew the interrogation would begin immediately when she arrived back home. They would want to know why she was doing this. Her dad had supported her and paid for a college education, but Megan knew he didn't want her to pursue a career involving animals. He felt that if a woman had to work, it should be a dignified job inside an office or a fancy shop. Men did the laborious stuff, like running a ranch, taking care of animals, and truck driving. As for her mother, since she had been a stay-at-home wife and mom her entire adult life, never having had an outside career, Megan was sure she would just go along with her dad's opinion.

This time, Megan didn't stop upon reaching the edge of the woods but kept her horse going at the same rapid pace until she arrived at the movie's base camp. There, she slowed down to a walk, since it was now a little after seven and already the area was bustling with activity. But with all the people moving about she decided it would be even wiser to dismount and walk her horse over to the corral. While doing all this, she surreptitiously looked for Gil. *He's probably in the tent eating breakfast*.

Reaching the corral, Megan spotted Eller talking to a woman who was trying to hand him several pieces of paper. He didn't seem pleased and, as she approached, Megan heard him say, "No, I don't want it done like that. Go back to that last scene and change it. And, please hurry. We're scheduled to film that segment this afternoon."

"Yes, Mr. Eller." The lady sounded contrite and quickly left. Megan could see that the director kept his crew constantly on their toes. He made sure that everyone knew, at all times, he was the one in control.

Eller's expression, seeing Megan standing there,

changed from irritation to pleasure. "Well, hello, young lady, you made good time. I appreciate your coming on such short notice to do this." With that, he took her arm and led her over to a small pen behind the large corral. "Here's the goat. How does he look to you?"

Megan reached down and, holding its chin, turned his head so that she could look at the eyes and then the mouth. She carefully looked over the rest of the goat's body too. Everything seemed normal. "Frankly, I can't find anything wrong, Paul. What was the problem you noticed?"

Eller looked sheepish as he asked, "Well, don't you notice that strange smell?"

"The smell?" Megan was confused. "What smell?"

"It's that strong odor coming from the animal. Surely, that can't be normal. Something must be wrong."

Stopping herself just in time, Megan almost burst out laughing. "I'm sorry, Paul, but that's the way all goats smell. Females aren't quite as bad and are more pleasant to have around. Really, I don't think there's anything wrong with this little critter."

"Wrong with what critter?" a voice said from behind. Turning, Megan and Eller saw Gil standing there, a strange, perplexed look on his face.

"Oh, hi Gil," said Megan while the director merely nodded his head.

"What are you doing with my goat?" asked Gil, who now seemed upset.

Megan waited, but Eller didn't say anything, so she tried to explain. "Paul thought the goat was ill, but before calling in a vet, he asked me to take a look at it. I did, and I believe the smell he was concerned about is normal for a male goat and that he doesn't need to call the vet. What do you think?"

Looking directly at Eller, Gil replied, "I don't believe my opinion is needed here is it, Paul?" Without waiting for an answer, Gil turned and walked away.

Megan could feel tension coming from both men but didn't know the cause. "What's his problem?" she asked the director, still standing beside her.

"Oh, I guess he's a little put out because I didn't call him to look at the goat, it being his animal and all. He usually takes care of these things, but I just thought I would spare him the trouble and called you, instead. I hope you don't mind?"

Megan didn't know what to think at the moment. Something was going on between the two men and she, like some innocent bystander, was being drawn into the middle of it. "Well, I guess since you now have my professional diagnosis, I'll head on home." In reality, she was afraid to hang around any longer, not knowing what would happen next.

"Thanks so much for your help, Megan. I really appreciate you coming so quickly. Would you mind if I called on you again some time?"

Frankly, she didn't know if she minded or not. But

being polite Megan told him that he could. His next question, however, was even tougher to answer.

"How about I reimburse you for your services by buying you dinner tonight?" Eller, now shedding his role as the businessman, had become flirtatious.

"Oh really, Paul, that's not necessary."

"Yes, it is. After all your help, it's the least I can do. I'll stop by your house around seven to pick you up, if that's all right."

"Okay," she answered meekly.

"Fine then, seven it is." And with a casual wave, Eller hurried off to a chauffeured car that was waiting for him. She watched it drive off, apparently headed for the movie set and then, mounting her horse, Megan prepared to leave. She was beginning to believe that she should have followed her father's orders and stayed entirely away from this base camp, the set, and any related movie dealings, especially the people involved.

Moving slowly, she left the corral, and circled the RV area, staying as far away from the catering tent as possible. She had no desire to cross paths or talk to any more of these people, at the moment. But, as she passed by, Megan noticed that several acknowledged her presence with a wave, or shouted out a greeting. Maybe some were beginning to recognize her from all these early morning appearances.

As she reached the outer limits of the camp, Gil came around the corner of a portable storage building and stood right in front of her. But, before he could say anything, she offered a quick apology. "I'm so sorry. I didn't know I was invading your turf, Gil. He just called this morning and asked me to come. I didn't know that it was your goat."

But Gil didn't lecture her. Instead, he said with a smile, "No problem, Megan. I was just surprised to see you here. I'm sure Eller had his reasons for calling you. Hey, if you have the time, would you like to go over to the catering tent and grab a quick cup of coffee with me?"

To say Megan was surprised would be putting it mildly. This was the last thing she expected. But since it was exactly what she wanted to do all along—go into that tent and check out the people—his offer was eagerly accepted.

Gil walked alongside as she rode her horse back to the corral and, tying the reins to a post, the two went over to the busy tent. After first standing in a short line for the coffee, they claimed one of the few empty tables left. Sitting there across from this ruggedly handsome guy and drinking from her cup, Megan noticed his large, competent hands. Her gaze then moved up to rest directly on his face, lingering in such a way that he looked over and smiled. From the moment they met, his obvious and intense awareness of her movements was evident, making him seem, in many ways, special and different from most guys.

While Gil still had most of her attention, Megan began checking out other people in the tent and then spotted the same man she had seen the day before, but couldn't identify. "Gil, who's that man three tables over? I recognize him, but can't come up with a name."

"You mean Wade Dillon? Why, he has the male lead in *Running Bull* and is the one I double for in the action scenes."

Then, Dillon looked over and saw Gil. Having finished his morning meal, the man stood and, after putting his plate and silverware back on the tray, he began walking toward them, something that rendered Megan speechless. But, Gil, who seemed entirely comfortable with all this said, "Hi, Wade, how's it going?"

"Not too bad, Gil, except for the sore knee I got yesterday when I fell off that porch. No problem, though. Today I'll be sitting most of the time, either behind a desk or at a table in the bar. Those are two of the scenes they're scheduled to shoot." Shifting his attention to Megan, the actor produced one of his celebrated smiles. "And who's this lovely lady?"

"Oh, this is Megan Wakefield," Gil answered. "Her dad owns this ranch we're filming on. And, Megan, this is Wade Dillon, star of the movie."

Dillon stuck out his hand which she quickly shook. "It's nice to meet you, Mr. Dillon," Megan said.

"Oh, call me Wade, and it's nice to meet you too. Hope we see more of you around here." Nodding his head toward Gil and extending a big smile to the room at large, Dillon went over to deposit his tray on the cart and, without anymore delays, left the tent. Megan's eyes followed the man until he disappeared.

But as she tried to refocus and give Gil her full attention, Megan was once again distracted, this time by a rapidly approaching Angela Taylor. "Gil, darling," the actress cooed, her interest entirely on him and ignoring Megan completely. "Don't forget tonight. I've already made a seven o'clock reservation for us at The Pines."

Megan watched as Gil came up with a weak, awkward smile. "Sure, Angela, I'll see you then." Before he could say anything more, the woman leaned over, kissed him on the cheek and then sauntered from the tent.

It was almost deafening, the silence that consumed their table. Megan wasn't quite sure what she wanted to say and Gil seemed embarrassed. Finally, he came up with an explanation. "Angela asked me yesterday if I'd have dinner with her tonight. She wants to discuss some script material."

"I see," answered Megan and let the subject drop. It wasn't long before her cup was empty, so standing up Megan prepared to leave. "Thanks, Gil, for the coffee, but I've got to run. When Paul called this morning, he got me out of bed, and I really need to get home and do my chores."

"Sure, Megan," Gil responded as he, too, got up. Putting their empty cups on the rack by the door, they left the tent, Megan heading toward the corral and her horse, Gil to his RV.

Chapter Four

It was almost ten o'clock when Megan reined her horse in behind the large, single-story wooden ranch house where she had grown up. After unsaddling the animal and placing it safely in one of the corrals, she went inside and found her mom and dad still drinking coffee, but this time in the living room as they watched a game show. Without hesitation, when Megan entered, Naomi turned the TV off. "Well, did you cure the animal?" her dad asked.

"No. Actually, there was nothing wrong except the poor thing smelled like any normal male goat, something Mr. Eller didn't realize, having never been around one before." All three laughed at this.

Then her mother asked, "Would you like a cup of coffee, dear?"

"No thanks, I just finished one back at base camp," and Megan went on to explain, in detail, her busy morning, including having had the opportunity to meet the famous actor, Wade Dillon. She added that Angela Taylor also stopped by their table, but left it at that.

Megan noticed that her dad seemed distracted, even worried, as she told them all this. So, quickly ending her story she asked him what was wrong. Surprised by her question and after a slight hesitation, Jim answered, "Oh, nothing."

Not knowing where to go from there, Megan looked over at her mom. "What's going on here?" she asked. Her mother just shook her head and, for the second time that day, she found herself surrounded by uncomfortable silence.

Finally, Jim spoke up. "Well, I guess I should tell you. Last week's check from the movie company hasn't arrived yet and today the next one is due. If I don't get this one on time, I won't be able to pay the bills and pretty soon we're going to be in deep trouble."

"Well, Dad, why don't you call Mr. Eller? Maybe there's been a mixup in the mail or something?" Megan could see that her father was quite concerned.

Jim got up from the couch and began to pace the floor. His daughter knew he took pride in paying his bills promptly and if unable to do so, he became terribly troubled and highly embarrassed.

"Yes, I guess I could do that. First, I'll wait and see if the checks come in today. But, if push comes to shove,

I'll call him." With that, her dad grabbed his cup up from the coffee table and took it back to the kitchen for a refill.

Megan, looking over at her mom, decided to change the subject. "Oh, by the way, Mr. Eller invited me out to dinner tonight. He said it was in payment for diagnosing his goat."

"That's nice, but from what you told us, it didn't sound like you did enough to earn a meal. Where will you be going to eat?"

"I don't know. He didn't tell me. But the problem is, and even though he didn't actually say so, he kept acting like this might be a date."

"That's odd. Isn't Mr. Eller considerably older than you?" asked Naomi.

"Oh, yes, he must be in his forties. But age doesn't seem to be a problem with these movie people. In fact, this whole business can sometimes make a person feel like they're in a fantasy world. They might take off the costume, but they all still keep playing their role."

"Are you going to go out with him?" She knew her mother wouldn't tell her what to do. Since returning from college, Megan had noticed that her mom was trying to accept the fact her daughter was an adult and should be allowed to make her own choices and decisions, even if Naomi didn't agree.

"No, I'm not going out with him, but I am going to dinner, which is different, at least in my mind." Megan was beginning to feel defensive. Although she knew her mother wasn't going to express an opinion, she was still curious as to what was going on in her head. Did her mom approve or disapprove of her having dinner with this man?

Megan doubted that her mom ever had to make a similar decision. After graduating from high school, Naomi and Jim married and then came to live in this big house with Jim's parents. Once again, Megan couldn't help but wonder why her mother had chosen a life so totally opposite from the one she wanted for her daughter. Were things so different back then that her mother had no choice except to stay in the background, doing only the cooking and cleaning?

Naomi had told Megan many stories about that first year, after moving in with the Wakefields. Right from the start, Naomi shared all the household duties with her mother-in-law until, that is, the following winter when the older Wakefield woman got pneumonia and died. Naomi, barely nineteen years old and six months pregnant with Megan, was left with the sole responsibility of maintaining the household. She was also expected to take care of and feed any animals that were corralled or penned out back.

The role Megan's dad played in all this, however, was just the opposite. He did the masculine jobs, the outside work with animals and land. And, Jim, his entire life, had looked forward to one day owning the ranch and assuming all the responsibilities that came with it. Even as a young, newly married man, his opinions had been strong and Jim made sure that everyone was well aware of them. This caused problems when his dad didn't agree, as often the older man's ideas and plans differed from those of his son. Megan, though a small child at the time, could still remember arguments, sometimes very heated ones, between the men.

Now, the grown daughter of Naomi and Jim, Megan sometimes wondered where she fit in this overall picture. Having inherited genes from both sides, her hope was to be a happy combination of both.

Suddenly, these strange thoughts were interrupted by Naomi who said, smiling, "My, my, two dinner dates in two days."

"Yes, and with two completely different men." Growing uncomfortable thinking about the upcoming meal with Eller, the girl got up from her chair and, using a feeble excuse, prepared to leave the room.

But not before her mother said, "You'll do just fine."

Yes, I will, thought Megan, back in her own room, perched on the edge of the bed, *but only if this silly dinner tonight comes with no strings attached.*

After leaving the catering tent that morning, Gil had gone to his RV, picked up a few things, and then went over to the corral where he saddled Geronimo. This time, he didn't have to visit wardrobe, makeup, or the prop trailer before going to the set since he would be spending the day working behind the scenes and off camera. The herd of longhorn cattle, scheduled to be filmed, was his only concern. Along with help from part-time wranglers, it would be his job to keep the animals moving and going in the right direction while, at the same time, staying out of camera range. And, of course, the crew filming the herd would also try not to record any of those behind-the-scene activities.

The day turned out to be a rare one, when everything went well with only a few glitches. So, during breaks, when Gil wasn't actively participating, he found his mind wandering back to earlier that morning and the time he had spent with Megan in the catering tent. Gil had no idea why so many of his thoughts or emotions, lately, involved her.

Of course, when he found Megan standing there at the pen with Eller, he had to admit he was furious. After all, these animals were his job, his concern, not hers. And, why would Eller call Megan in the first place and not him? But, when seeing her about to leave the camp, he knew that all he really wanted was to be with her, to talk to her. So on impulse, he had invited the girl to go over to the food tent for coffee and, to his amazement, she accepted without hesitation.

And that had gone smoothly, too, until Angela showed up and behaved so rudely, ignoring Megan's presence. Any sense of togetherness he and the girl might have felt toward each other came to an abrupt halt. This was the same thing that had happened the night before at Toby's when Eller appeared. However, Gil promised himself that if given a third chance to be alone with Megan, he would do his best to prevent anything or anyone else from ruining it.

These thoughts were quickly put on hold, however, when Gil again heard his name being called. Apparently, they were ready to begin the shoot once more and he needed to get the cattle moving. So, for the next several hours, he and the wranglers had their hands full. Even though it was hard work and required a great deal of energy, Gil would still rather be doing this on the movie set than on a ranch. Luckily, the filming went well and when Eller yelled, "That's a wrap!" everyone seemed pleased.

As Gil was about to mount Geronimo and head back to camp, he heard some loud female voices coming from behind him. Turning, he saw Angela and her stunt double, Kim, engaged in a rather heated argument. Though he couldn't actually hear the words, the tone of voice and body language of the women wasn't good. Creating a film, under the best of circumstances, was hard enough without throwing in anger and volatile confrontations among its participants. Then he had an idea. *I wonder if Megan ever thought of doing stunt-double work.* With all her animal skills, vet training, and being able to ride a horse so well, he felt that after some training, Megan could do it just fine. Now convinced of that, he'd see if she was interested.

The evening was clear and pleasant as the chauffeured limo pulled up and parked in front of The Pines

Restaurant. The driver went around and opened the door for Megan and Paul Eller.

"You don't have to wait for us here, Frank, but be sure and return no later than eight-thirty," the director instructed. Taking Megan's arm, he escorted her into the town's most plush dining establishment.

Upon entering, the two were taken to their reserved table and given a menu. Megan had been to The Pines only once before, and that was the night of her high school graduation. Although eating there made her feel special, she always felt this restaurant was a little too pricey for her family's pocketbook. And, actually, Megan preferred the steaks at Toby's. Plus, as she discovered, she was unfamiliar with all the foreign words used to identify some of the items on the menu.

Realizing this, Eller suggested she order a dish with some fancy French name that turned out to be baked ham served with potatoes and cheese. He ordered the same thing for himself along with whiskey on the rocks, as opposed to the iced tea Megan chose to drink.

Sitting there, the napkin in her lap, Megan began to feel uncomfortable as Eller, drink in hand, stared at her, a strange smile on his face. Then, he began asking questions about her life in general and her four years of school. Though trying to appear interested in her degree in animal care, he seemed more intent on discovering the extent of her business knowledge. Finally, Megan decided that not only was this guy old enough to be her father, he was beginning to sound just like him.

Matters only got worse. At the same moment the waiter appeared with their dinner, Megan saw Angela walk through the main entrance followed by Gil, and she remembered the actress saying something that morning about meeting Gil at The Pines for dinner. Though this restaurant hadn't been Megan's choice, she felt foolish being there and hoped the couple wouldn't see her and sit across the room.

Of course, this didn't happen. In fact, they walked right by Megan before being seated only two tables away. While this didn't seem to faze the director, Megan saw that Angela wasn't at all pleased, and would have just gone on by without acknowledging their presence, except Eller called out her name.

So, once again, totally ignoring Megan, Angela uttered a curt "Hello, Paul," as she grabbed Gil's arm and dragged him over to their table. Gil, on the other hand, seemed as though he wanted to talk to Megan and explain things, but other than a quick, "Hi, Megan," was never given the opportunity.

Now, picking up her fork to begin eating, Megan realized that Eller seemed almost gleeful. Did he know Angela and Gil would be having dinner at The Pines that evening and, if so, did he want to be found there with someone else? It certainly seemed that way, especially when she noticed him glancing frequently over toward the actress' table. And, when Angela finally looked in their direction, he reached for Megan's hand and tried to make it appear as if something romantic was going on between them. *What is all this about?* Megan wondered.

Having watched Eller's keen interest in Angela and then his strange behavior, Megan began to suspect he was romantically interested in the woman; that he had only invited her out to dinner that night to try and make Angela jealous. But, if that was the case, it didn't seem to be working. In fact, just the opposite was taking place. Though he managed to conceal his emotions fairly well, Megan could see that Angela's appearance with Gil had produced instead, a strong jealous response from Eller.

By now, and though the meal was appetizing, Megan had become extremely uncomfortable and couldn't wait for the evening to end. But during dessert Eller brought up a subject that did catch her attention. "Have you ever thought of doing film work?" he asked.

"Well, not until this morning when you called me to check out the goat," she answered honestly.

"No, I mean, have you ever thought about acting, appearing on camera, maybe as an extra, or possibly something more?"

Now he did have her attention. "No, I can't say that I have, but it sounds interesting." Megan began to feel more relaxed and started to enjoy the evening.

"Well, if you're interested, show up on the set tomorrow at eight o'clock and I just might have some temporary acting work for you."

"Will I get paid for it?" Megan was thinking that if

she did make some money, she could help out her dad with the household expenses.

"You sure will. And, who knows, maybe this will lead to even bigger and better things." Eller glanced over at the other table, apparently checking to see if Angela had noticed the big smile now on Megan's face. She hadn't.

Finally, the meal ended and Eller asked if she was ready to leave. Megan, who had been more than ready for quite some time murmured a polite, "Yes".

Little was said in the limo on their way back to the ranch, but when he walked her up to the front door Eller, once again, reminded Megan to be on the set first thing the following morning. Then, leaning over, he planted a fleeting kiss on her lips. Completely caught off guard, she didn't respond in either a favorable or negative way but, instead, merely stood there watching as he walked down the steps and back to the waiting vehicle.

Chapter Five

After a night of fitful sleep, Megan was up, dressed and ready to go long before her alarm went off. Entering the kitchen, she discovered her mother was also up and had the coffee made, so Megan paused long enough to drink a cup, accompanied by a slice of homemade coffee cake. Bubba came over to sit on the floor beside her, eager for food scraps or a friendly scratch behind the ears.

"Well, I see you got up in plenty of time for your first day as a movie star," said Naomi, who had always been an early riser.

"Oh, yes, and I'm so excited!"

Megan ate quickly, finally stuffing the last bite of coffee cake into her mouth and washing it down with coffee. Not only was she trying to get to the set on time, she also didn't want to be in the kitchen when her dad arrived. She was tired of listening to his all too familiar negative comments about the film industry.

Arriving home after her dinner episode with Eller, Megan had found her parents still up and watching television in the living room. Unable to wait, she told them about being offered a job as an extra. While her mom seemed to go along with the idea, her dad was hesitant. Apparently, the second lease check had not arrived and Jim was getting a bit anxious about this whole movie-business thing.

Grabbing her jacket, Megan now went out the side door and into the garage where she found the family's all-terrain vehicle. Though used for ranch work, she figured it would be a more professional ride than her horse and, before long she arrived at the camp area and drove to the set.

Although still quite early, a great deal of activity was already in progress and Megan, not seeing anyone she recognized, wondered what to do next. Then, just as she was about to turn around and drive back to base camp in the hope of maybe finding someone there to talk to, a van drove up, stopping not far away. Paul Eller got out, followed by Angela Taylor and another man she didn't recognize. Only then did she see Gil, partially hidden behind a large covered wagon, sitting atop his horse. At the same moment he recognized her, waved and a cheerful smiled flashed across his face. Megan quickly responded with one of her own as

Eller walked up and said, "Hey, I'm glad to see you made it."

Turning to look at Eller, Megan noticed Angela and the other man still standing over by the van, watching them. Megan also noticed the actress didn't seem pleased. Had Angela seen her just exchange waves with Gil and was jealous? Or was she upset at the attention Megan was getting from Eller? The girl didn't have a clue.

So, she simply responded with, "Hi, Paul, yes, I made it. Is there something you want me to do today?" His answer, however, wasn't what she expected.

"Well, not today. But I think we can use you as an extra in a scene being filmed tomorrow. That is, if you want to." Glancing over to make sure Angela was watching, Eller reached out and put his arm around Megan's shoulders. *Just what kind of game is this guy playing?* Although disappointed that he didn't need her right then, but still pleased at the prospect of acting in a real movie the next day, she asked, "What time do you want me here?"

"Well, you'll need to be at the base camp around five in the morning. You'll have to go to the wardrobe trailer first and get your costume. I'll tell them that you're coming and what to give you. Then, after you get dressed, go over to makeup and let them prepare you for the scene. When you're finished with that, come here to the set. Can you remember all this or should I have someone meet you tomorrow morning and walk you through it?"

"No, you don't have to do that. I know my way around the camp pretty well now and if I have any questions, I'm sure I can find someone who can answer them."

"Good girl! Well, I've got to go. We're already running late this morning." With that, Eller hurried back over to Angela, still at the same spot by the van and wearing a frown on her perfect face. The other man had disappeared.

While not understanding any of this, Megan pushed these strange interactions between star and director from her mind and decided to hang around and watch for a while. After parking her car safely out of the way, she was walking back toward the set when her attention was captured by another chauffeured vehicle. It drove slowly past her, stopped only a short distance away and Wade Dillon, the movie's hero, got out. The big surprise came, however, when he turned and waited for Megan to approach. "Hey, little lady," he called out, "what are you doing here so early?"

Clearing her throat, Megan finally managed a nervous "Hello." Then, trying once more and in a stronger voice, she said, "Paul Eller asked me to come. I'm going to be an extra tomorrow and he needed to tell me what to do and where to go."

"Great! Tomorrow, you say? Hey, that's the saloon

scene so you'll probably be one of the bar girls. You know, one of the hookers that hang out there."

She was shocked. Megan had just assumed she would be wearing a long western dress and big bonnet while walking down the dirt road of the fake town, maybe even pretending to shop. Not once had she pictured herself as a prostitute, wearing some kind of skimpy outfit. The idea, though a little daunting, was at the same time rather challenging and she knew she wouldn't be mentioning this to her mom and dad. Someone called out Dillon's name. So, after telling Megan to enjoy herself, he hurried off.

The rest of the morning flew by. Megan stayed in the background, watching closely as several short scenes were filmed and even learned a few things about the acting business. Then Megan felt a tap on her shoulder and heard Gil ask, "Are you enjoying yourself?"

Turning quickly, she answered, "I sure am. This is all so fascinating. And that part where you fell off the horse was unbelievable!"

"Have you ever fallen from a horse?"

"Oh yes, several times, but it hurt and apparently yours didn't, or at least not too much." Megan remembered her most recent fall, several months earlier, and it hadn't been any fun at all.

"Would you like to learn how to do it safely?"

Curious, Megan wondered just where this conversation was going. "Why? Do you want to teach me?" she asked in a teasing manner.

Though still smiling, Gil left no doubt that his answer was to be taken seriously. "Yes. So, how about meeting me this afternoon out in the pasture near the back woods?"

Without even thinking, a surprised Megan answered, "Sure. That sounds like fun. Should I bring my horse?"

"Under the circumstances, it probably would be a good idea," Gil said, jokingly.

Now, Megan felt like a real fool. Of course if she was going to learn how to fall from it she would need her horse. Gil's name was called out just then over the loudspeaker. After a hasty good-bye and his reminder to meet at three o'clock, Gil hurried off and Megan decided that she had watched enough filming for one day. Then, while walking to her ATV, she saw Angela standing off in the distance, glaring at her.

Promptly at three o'clock that afternoon, Gil and Geronimo arrived at the pasture. The day was warm and sunny, in the low seventies, with only a light breeze. He couldn't have asked for anything better or have been more pleased, especially when he looked up and saw Megan coming toward him at full gallop.

It was like the opening scene of a movie, only there was no musical score reaching a brilliant crescendo as she rode up and stopped; except, that is, in his heart. *Stop it. You're acting like a teenager on his first date.* These thoughts, however, brought a warm, red glow to his face which embarrassed him.

"Hey," said Megan, "you beat me here." She looked so appealing and vivacious sitting atop the animal, reining it in.

"Yeah, my part in the shoot went well and I got off even earlier than I had figured." He didn't go on to explain that he would have arrived even sooner except Angela had stopped him just as he was about to leave the set.

"Hello, Gil," the actress had said grabbing his arm and gently rubbing her body against his. "How about hanging around a little while longer and then we'll go into town and have a drink?"

Surprised by the offer, but definitely not interested, he had removed, as politely as possible, her hand from his arm and stepped backwards. "I'm sorry, Angela, but I've made other plans and I've got to get going if I'm going to be on time." He could still remember her unpleasant look just before they heard Eller call out, "Angela, we're about to shoot. Can you please get back over here now?" Gil thought the director sounded even more gruff and abrupt than usual.

"Sorry, Angela," Gil said again to the actress, who hadn't moved or even acknowledged Eller's command. "Maybe some other time, but I'm due to meet someone over by the woods in about ten minutes."

Angela didn't move but he did. Reaching out, Gil had grabbed the reins to his horse and quickly left the set. He really didn't know if he was hurrying to his appointment with Megan or running to get away from Angela. However, these thoughts stopped as he looked up at Megan. "Hi, Gil," she said with a big grin.

Megan's natural beauty was charged with youthful energy and her eyes sparkled in anticipation. Though she seemed excited about being there and learning some new horse tricks, Megan also seemed calm and in control as she stroked the animal's head.

It was a good looking horse and Gil could tell by the way she handled it that the animal already had some training. Just how much, he couldn't say. To do that, he would actually have to mount and ride it.

"Hi, yourself." He held onto the horse as she climbed down out of the saddle to stand in front of him. Their eyes locked and held for a moment—a look that had the kick of a mule. Suddenly, all he wanted to do was snatch her up into his arms and hold on forever, but he resisted. Instead, he led the horse some distance away, more for his benefit than that of the animal. However, Megan followed.

I've got to get a grip. She came here to learn about horses and this has nothing to do with me, personally . . . but I wish it did.

Although the horse appeared to be trained and controllable, it wasn't long before Gil realized it wasn't ready to be a fall horse. So he asked Megan to take the reins and lead Geronimo around for a while. This would give them a chance to get acquainted. As she did this, Gil noticed Megan seemed to be a natural around horses and her commanding manner kept the animal's attention. After a while, Gil asked her to mount Geronimo. In spite of her small stature, Megan got up into the saddle quickly, but Gil did have to shorten the stirrups. Then, while he watched, Gil had her ride around the pasture so that she and the horse could become better acquainted.

She began with a walk and, when comfortable enough, she nudged the horse's flank with the heel of her boot, urging it into a gallop. Gil was impressed. Megan did seem to have a way with horses. However, while watching these proceedings something else caught his eye, if only for a moment. It was a flash of light coming from the woods bordering the pasture, as if the sun's rays had just reflected off glass or metal. *Could it be binoculars? Is someone out there watching us?* But, it only happened that once and although he looked over several more times, Gil didn't see anyone or anything else.

Finally, it was time for the big test. Originally, he had planned to teach Megan how to make her own horse fall. But now he knew that even though her horse was well trained it really wasn't skilled enough to handle this. These things usually, but not always, had to be learned early in an animal's life.

So mounting Geronimo, and as Megan watched, Gil galloped out a short distance into the pasture. Turning, he had the animal run back toward Megan. He showed her how to pull the horse's head sharply back and to the side with the reins, causing the horse to position its front legs straight out in front, while automatically falling onto its side. He also showed Megan where her own legs should be and where to put her body when this happened. Gil demonstrated all of this a second time before Megan, having readjusted the stirrups, got up into the saddle and tried it herself.

The first time she was a bit hesitant when pulling the horse's head to the side and the animal, staying on its feet, merely walked around in a narrow circle. On the next attempt, however, she yanked the reins hard enough and the horse immediately extended its legs and went down on its side, taking Megan with him. Gil held his breath. It looked like a good fall, but he really couldn't tell until he got up close and could see that Megan was uninjured. In fact, she was lying on the ground, laughing. Bringing the horse back to its feet, Gil kneeled down beside her as she, at that exact moment, sat up, her lips only inches away from his.

Gil's original intent for being there on the ground next to Megan was to offer strength and comfort as any teacher would. This plan, however, quickly changed as he leaned forward, eliminating the inches separating them, and covered her lips with his. He tasted her full red lips, savored her scent, and soon it all became a part of him, a memory that would last forever. He felt her reach up and put her arms around his neck and, while a gesture of trust, it caused him to panic. *What are we doing?*

Pulling his lips away from hers before it could go

any further, Gil once again caught a glimpse of the same reflected light coming from the woods. *Is someone watching us?* Quickly, he answered his own question, *No way! Who would want to do that?* Anyway, the only person he had told about this meeting was Angela and why would she sneak into the woods and watch through binoculars?

Taking no chances, though, he reached for Megan's hand and pulled her back on her feet. Neither mentioned nor referred to the exquisite kiss. He managed to ask if she wanted to try the fall again.

"No, I think I've had enough excitement for one day," Megan said, apparently not realizing, until she saw Gil's mouth angle into a half smile, that this statement could have had several meanings. Trying to clarify this, she said, "What I meant to say is, since the sun is setting, I'd better get back home. Mom will have dinner ready shortly."

Trying to be a gentleman and not laugh at her obvious discomfort, Gil assured her that she was right. It was getting too dark to try to do any more that day. Actually, what he wanted to do was invite her out to dinner or, better still, over to his RV where they could spend some time alone. Maybe next time, and he sincerely hoped there would be a next time very soon.

Chapter Six

The alarm next to Megan's bed went off at a hideously early hour but she didn't mind. In fact, she was eager to begin her first day as a movie star. Well, maybe not a star, at least, not yet.

Dressing quickly, she headed for the kitchen but her mother wasn't there and neither was the coffee. This was the first time that she could remember ever getting up before Naomi, and Megan was somewhat concerned until she realized just how early it was. Although disappointed, as she had hoped to begin her day with a hot cup of coffee, Megan knew she could always get one at the catering tent.

Catering tent, base camp, Megan was amazed at how quickly she was learning this film industry lingo. Even though she had always been a good student, school had never been this easy, this much fun, or as bewildering. Lately, Megan had become a lot less sure as to what was her real career choice. However, one thing she did know was that her parents wouldn't be happy if she picked the movies. In fact, her mother was still urging her to read the want ads and apply for office work.

As these thoughts kept mounting, so did the guilt. In order to get some relief, Megan made herself a promise. Even though movie work was more exciting, she would start sending out at least one resume every day to a regular business, the kind her parents would approve of. And, she would begin that afternoon, doing just that.

Again using the ATV, she managed to reach base camp only a few minutes after five. Megan had a general idea where she was going, but did stop once to ask someone for directions to wardrobe. She thought she had prepared herself emotionally for the saloon girl costume. The shock, though, when she emerged from the dressing room and caught sight of her semi-naked body, fully displayed on the wall mirror, was far greater than she had anticipated. Several other people inside the trailer also saw her, but no one appeared stunned or surprised, though two men did stare at her in a more personal way. Apparently, seeing someone in a skimpy costume wasn't a new experience and even if she had appeared before the group completely naked, it would have been just another day on the movie set.

From there, she went over to makeup and after a half hour of preparation, came out of the trailer in full battle array. Lips lined in scarlet and filled in with ruby-red color, eyes accentuated in various shades of blacks and blues with a hint of glitter, and cheeks rosy enough to make even a young child envious, was more makeup than she'd worn in a lifetime.

Avoiding any further contact with her reflection in the mirrors, she ran to the ATV, got on, and headed for the movie set. Though it was not yet seven-thirty and Megan knew she had time to stop by the catering tent for coffee, she was still too embarrassed to be seen out in public, dressed in such attire. Realizing this, Megan began to laugh. *Yes, I'm too self-conscious to go into that tent where there's probably others in similar outfits, but I'm not too embarrassed to go over to the set and let them put my image on film and then send it out for the whole world to see.*

Though the day was just beginning, Megan wasn't the first to arrive. Far from it! There were several other vehicles already outside the fabricated western town where she parked her ATV.

After first donning a jacket to help hide her nakedness, Megan attempted to walk nonchalantly and inconspicuously toward a group of people gathered at the end of the fake town's main street. However, no one seemed even remotely shocked upon seeing her half-hidden, semi-naked condition.

She looked around but recognized no one, even Gil, the one person she really wanted to see. He had been on her mind constantly since leaving the pasture, each going their separate way. This seemed to be the theme of their friendship. When they were about to grow closer, something always happened, causing them to head off in opposite directions.

Just as she was reaching her destination, the town saloon, a chauffeured vehicle drove down the main street and passed her. Stars and other important people didn't have to park outside the set and walk in. The car stopped a short ways down the road where most of the action seemed to be taking place, and Angela Taylor emerged, again dressed in black pants and a silver shirt. Before starting off toward the others who, by this time, were watching the celebrity approach, she looked over at Megan, her expression clearly that of anger or dislike.

What's her problem? Megan asked herself again. *Just what is it that I've done to upset her so much? She couldn't be jealous of my having dinner with Paul Eller, could she? After all, she was with Gil. Or, maybe my feelings for Gil are obvious and that's what's upsetting her.* These troubling questions replaced all the earlier feelings of embarrassment about her costume.

Reaching the front porch of the tavern where a crudely painted wooden sign, SALOON, hung out front, she saw several other girls in outfits similar to her own: fishnet stockings, skimpy satin skirts, and low-cut tops. The only difference between them and her was their apparent relaxed comfort in the costumes.

"Megan." Hearing her name, she turned to find Paul Eller coming through the bar's swinging doors. "Glad I caught you." Leading her off to the side, Paul gave her a visual once-over. "My goodness, girl, you look terrific."

This came as a surprise to Megan. Not so much his comments on her appearance, but the fact that he was being sociable. Megan hadn't been around the movie business that much, but long enough to know that when Eller was under pressure, or directing a shoot, he could seem uptight and even downright unfriendly. Now he was acting just the opposite.

"Thank you, Paul. But I'm really not sure what I'm supposed to do in there."

"Don't worry. You just have to walk around in front of the camera with the other girls. Maybe stop and tap the shoulder of a man seated at a table or standing at the bar; you know, to attract his attention. Then, you smile at him in a sexy, come-hither way. You can do that, can't you?"

Eller's penetrating gaze caused Megan to glance down at the ground, rendering her speechless. However, when looking up again, she found the director staring across the road at Angela. Seeing the actress glance in their direction, something he apparently had been waiting for, Eller reached out, pulled Megan into his arms, and gave her an endearing hug. Before she could respond in any way, he released her and then walked off, leaving Megan to stand there alone, mouth gaping, and thoroughly confused.

She was rescued from further embarrassment when her name was called out. One of the assistants, in a loud voice, had read it off a sheet of paper, along with several others. Running over to the bar's swinging doors Megan entered the building along with five other costumed girls.

It was a busy set. Besides Eller, the camera crew, and miscellaneous staff members, there were several male actors and extras dressed in western outfits, either standing at a long wooden bar or seated at rustic tables, playing cards. Everyone seemed relaxed and reasonably comfortable except for the director who, in a gruff and demanding voice, began instructing each girl where to stand, where to walk, and what to do.

Megan, by now, was no longer feeling embarrassed or uncomfortable in her scanty costume. In fact, she was beginning to enjoy being a part of this imaginary world. When her turn came, Eller approached and told her to stroll along behind three men at the bar, running her fingers lightly across their shoulders as she passed. Megan had no trouble doing this or anything else the director asked, even when she was instructed to smile seductively and act a little sassy. He watched her do all this twice and, after nodding his head in approval, moved on to coach the next extra posing as a prostitute. Before long, cameras began to roll and the first take was in progress. This three-minute scene was shot four separate times, after which the five girls were dismissed.

As they were leaving, a woman stopped them by the swinging doors and told them they might be called back to do a new scene or another take on the one just completed. Also, she asked them to hand in their signed vouchers and checks would be mailed out within a few weeks. Assuming the role of mother or perhaps governess, the woman firmly reminded the girls to go back to base camp right away and turn in their costumes. Megan, still feeling excited at having performed in her very first movie, began to giggle as she glanced over at one of the extras walking beside her.

"Hi," Megan said.

The girl answered "Hi" back.

Encouraged, Megan asked, "Have you ever done this before?"

"What? Be a hooker?" she responded with humor.

"No, appear in a movie?" Megan was still surprised that she, herself, had done this.

"Oh, this is my fifth time as an extra and I'm hoping to get a bit-part soon."

"Are you from around here?" Megan didn't know why she was asking all these questions. Maybe, she didn't want to let go of the morning's thrill.

"No. Right now I live in San Antonio, but I have a friend in Austin who lets me stay with her when I'm working in the area. Are you from around here?"

"Yes. This is my dad's ranch. Say, do you need a lift back to camp and the wardrobe trailer? I've got an ATV parked just outside the set and I'll be glad to give you a ride."

"Yeah, thanks. I came over in the courtesy van with some of the others but I'd much rather go back with you now and not have to wait."

So after Tracy Meeks introduced herself, as did Megan, the two left the set. It was almost noon and people were coming and going. However, Megan saw no sign of Gil, who probably wasn't there since the scenes being shot that morning were all inside, with no need for riders or livestock.

Back at camp, they headed for wardrobe to return their costumes. This took a little while as several other people were ahead of them, either returning what they already had or getting something new. Then, Tracy suggested they go and grab a bite to eat at the catering tent. By this time, Megan, having had no breakfast, was ravenous and agreed enthusiastically.

The tent was almost full but Megan spotted Gil immediately, sitting alone at a table. He was facing the other way and didn't see her arrive. Megan wanted to run over and join him but, knowing she couldn't abandon Tracy, she went through the line and, after selecting a tuna salad sandwich for lunch, followed her new acquaintance over to one of the few empty tables.

Even though conversation with Tracy was interesting, it seemed to take forever to get through the meal. Megan couldn't concentrate on anything except the guy sitting one row over and several tables down. But after a while Gil got up preparing to leave, and Megan was very much aware of the exact moment when he looked over and recognized her. Seeing that she wasn't alone didn't stop him from coming over to their table either.

"Hi, Megan," Gil said. Then, looking at her companion he asked, "And who's this?"

"Tracy Meeks." She stood up and held out her hand to shake his; all this before Megan could even open her mouth and make an introduction.

"Glad to meet you, Tracy," was his polite reply. "I'm Gil."

This was followed by a, "Will you join us?" again from Tracy, who was still standing.

"No, thanks, I just finished lunch and was leaving when I saw Megan and wanted to say hello. Nice meeting you, Tracy."

"Nice meeting you too," said Tracy who reclaimed her chair.

Looking at Megan, Gil asked, "What have you been up to this morning?"

"Oh, we spent some time being hookers," said Tracy, again interrupting. Both girls laughed as they watched a bizarre look cross Gil's face.

Megan added, "We were extras, called to act as saloon girls this morning. And I think the shoot went quite well, don't you, Tracy?"

"Yes, except for that one bimbo who kept moving over and blocking me from the camera. It happened so often, I bet I won't be seen at all when the picture comes out."

Megan wasn't aware of any of this going on. But, then so engrossed was she in playing her own part, she never would have noticed.

"What do you do around here, Gil?" Tracy asked, her provocative voice sounding, Megan thought, like a real prostitute. By now, she was becoming a trifle disconcerted. Was Tracy coming on to Gil? He didn't seem to be aware of this, or even of Megan's uneasiness.

Always eager to talk about his work, Gil replied, "I'm head wrangler and take care of the animals. I double as a stuntman for Wade Dillon too."

"Oh," Tracy cooed, "that's so exciting."

Not knowing what to say or think, Megan sat quietly, observing and listening to the idle chatter. And Tracy, who seemed completely unaware of her lunch partner's discomfort, continued. "Have you been doing this long?"

"For a while now," he answered before turning to Megan. "Well, I've got to run, but can I call you later?" She nodded "Yes" and after a, "Nice meeting you, Tracy," Gil left the tent.

"He's the stunt double for Wade Dillon?" Tracy asked. She not only seemed impressed, but also very interested.

"Yes," was Megan's abbreviated reply. By this time, all she wanted to do was leave, too, and get away from Tracy. *And, no, I'm not jealous,* Megan kept telling herself.

But she had to endure several more minutes of watching Tracy finish her sandwich before she could leave. Then, making as polite an exit as possible, Megan rose from the table and said, "Nice meeting you."

"Same here," the girl replied. Then, spotting someone across the room she wanted to speak to, Tracy said good-bye.

Megan left the tent and, while on her way to the edge of camp and her ATV, she passed several people, none of whom she recognized. So, it was a complete surprise when she heard, "Hey, Megan, what's your rush?"

Turning, she saw Gil running toward her. This unexpected second encounter caused instantaneous heart flutters. He certainly was a charmer and she found his manner quite seductive.

"Hi there," she called out. And when he arrived, added, "I'm not in any hurry, but since I was through here, I thought I'd head on home. What were you doing all morning?"

"Taking care of animals mostly," he answered.

"Oh?" Now, with her veterinary interest piqued, Megan asked if there was a problem with Geronimo or one of the others. Gil quickly assured her that all was fine and the day's activities had been routine. Then the conversation ended, with neither knowing what to say next.

"Well, I guess I'd better go." The words sounded lame and talking like this, how could she ever hope to attract a man like Gil? But, she asked herself, *Do I even want to? Yes,* was her immediate mental response, *yes, I do*!

Gil took her hand. "How come you're in such a rush to leave?" He didn't act at all put off by her poor choice of words or seeming lack of conversation. In fact, as he stared into her eyes, with his face growing closer, she knew he wasn't focusing on her voice, just her lips.

Thank goodness for that, she thought as she stuttered out another mindless answer. “Well, I’m not really in a rush. But they finished the bar scene and don’t need me anymore.”

These senseless remarks didn’t seem to put him off either and, after another quick lookaround, Gil moved even closer. However, before he could place his lips on hers, a voice called out, halting his intentions.

“Gil, could you come over here, please?” Gil and Megan separated and both turned to see Angela Taylor standing by the wardrobe trailer, waving her hand back and forth as if urging Gil to hurry.

Instead of rushing off in the star’s direction, Gil just continued to stand there, holding Megan’s hand. Calling out, he asked, “What do you need, Angela?”

“I need your help, Gil, right now. It’s my horse.” Placing one hand on her hip and waving the other in the air, Angela stood there, her eyes fully focused on Gil.

Megan could tell that Gil was irritated. “Well, I guess I’d better go see what she wants. Do you think we can meet later?” Before Megan could answer, Angela called out again and, shaking his head, Gil walked off in the star’s direction.

As she watched him leave, Megan realized any reason she may have had for staying at the camp had just left too. So, taking the keys from her pocket, she got onto the ATV and drove home, going her way once more as he went his.

Chapter Seven

For the next two days, Megan received no requests for more movie work, so Jim took advantage of this free time. He needed her help rounding up cows and herding them into the corral. Then, one by one, they gave each animal their yearly vaccination shot. For someone who thought women should work indoors, Wakefield certainly was keeping his daughter busy outside. And she didn't mind at all.

During this time, she also sent out two resumes in an attempt to pacify her mom. Both of them had been for office jobs and none as a vet's assistant, the work she had really wanted to pursue until this movie gig came along.

By the third day, Megan had to drag herself out of bed. She still had received no word or contact from anyone . . . not the movies or businesses she had submitted the resumes to. She commanded herself to stop fretting. *You had a good life before that movie crew came here and you don't need them now.*

Trying to remain focused and positive, Megan dug out some clean clothes and quickly dressed. Sprinting down the hallway, she popped into the kitchen and tried to come up with a convincing smile for her parents as she joined them at the table. It worked, as both returned her morning greeting.

"What's your schedule for today?" Jim asked, finishing his second slice of toast, coated with butter and jelly.

"Nothing so far; do you need me to help with something?"

"Not really. But, I do have to go into town and pick up some parts for the tractor. I thought maybe you'd like to ride along." Apparently her parents had noticed her recent lack of interest in anything except the movie, even though she enjoyed helping her dad and working with the animals. However, a trip to town did sound like a good way to pass some of the day.

"Sure, Dad, I'd love to ride along." Looking over at her mom, she asked, "Do we need to pick up any groceries?"

"Probably bread and milk but let me check and see. If necessary, I'll make a list, but a short one. With money getting scarce around here, we shouldn't buy anything we don't absolutely need."

Megan looked surprised. "We're still short on money?"

"Yeah, we haven't gotten a check from that movie company in almost three weeks," Jim said. "I guess I need to talk to them, but I don't know who to call. I suppose I could look over that contract we signed and see if I can come up with a name." So, right then, while he was thinking about it, Jim got up and walked down the hall to his office to get the contract.

Megan, trying to be helpful, offered to load the dishwasher and clean up the kitchen and Naomi quickly accepted. Megan knew her mother wanted to get started on the laundry as it was Wednesday, story-hour day, when Naomi read to pre-school children at the library. Four years ago, after Megan went off to college her mom had started doing this, surprising both daughter and husband. They never thought she would actually volunteer to go out and read in public. However, her mom was still at it and seemed to look forward to going each week.

Cleaning up the kitchen didn't take long and just as Megan finished, her dad returned, contract in hand.

"Oliver Plum signed on behalf of the film company," Jim said. "Since he's in California and, time-wise, there's a two-hour difference, he probably isn't in his office yet. I'll just wait until we get back from town to call him."

The mid-morning traffic was almost non-existent until Jim turned onto Main Street. He drove two more blocks before pulling into the usually full, but now quite empty hardware store parking lot. Megan had lost most of her morning's contrived enthusiasm and told her dad that she'd just wait in the pickup while he went inside to buy some parts.

She'd been sitting there only a few minutes when, hearing a tap on the window beside her, Megan literally jumped. Turning, she saw Paul Eller motioning her to roll it down. Instead, she opened the door and got out.

"Hi. What are you doing here?" Megan asked. Not very polite, but this was the best response she could come up with.

"They needed some tools and since we're not scheduled to film until noon, I decided to let the others sleep in for a change and come get them myself. But, what are you doing sitting out here all alone?" He gave her his well rehearsed smile, one that was supposed to generate some sort of attraction.

"Oh, my dad had to pick up some tractor parts. And it shouldn't take long so I just decided to wait here."

"Lucky for me that you did," he responded, before conveying another enticing smile.

Just then, her dad approached and Megan was saved from more senseless conversation. "Hey, Eller," Jim said, "You're just the man I wanted to see."

Megan watched the director replace his come-hither smile with a casual grin before turning to shake hands with Jim. That's when Megan decided movie people never really left the set or stopped acting, completely. They just responded to real-life situations as they had been taught to do for a specific part in a script. And, the strange thing was, she couldn't decide if this was good or bad. All Megan knew for sure was that she wanted to be a part of it.

"What can I do for you?" Eller asked.

"Well, for openers, you can pay up what you owe me."

Megan detected a hint of anger in her dad's voice and saw Eller struggling for the right response. He chose an indignant attitude.

"You mean to tell me those fools back in California haven't gotten this mess straightened out yet? Why, only yesterday they assured me that they had. But don't worry, Jim. I'll give them a call as soon as I get back to camp and you'll have your money shortly, I promise."

"Good. Because when I get back home, I'm giving Mr. Plum a call too. If this isn't straightened out soon, I'm canceling the contract and you'll be off my land in twenty-four hours. That check, for the full amount, had better be in my mailbox by Monday or, so help me, you're history."

Megan knew that her dad meant every word and she could see, by his expression, Eller was aware of this too.

"Don't worry, Jim, you'll have it by then, maybe even sooner." Eller now looked directly at Megan's dad, donning his most sincere, yet businesslike expression. "There's been a computer glitch somewhere but I'll get on the phone right away and see that this matter is cleared up once and for all."

"Good. I certainly hope so. I really don't want to get ugly, but I'll be forced to if I don't get paid."

"Now, now, as I said before, don't worry, Jim. I'll get this taken care of immediately."

Eller, eager to change the subject, turned to Megan. "Oh, I was going to ask you earlier, Megan, if you would be interested in working as Angela's double and stunt girl for the remainder of the shoot. Kim, the girl who was doing it, was called away unexpectedly. Since you seem comfortable around horses and are somewhat similar in size and appearance to Angela, by wearing a red wig, I figured you'd be perfect for the job. Of course, your pay for this work will be a lot more than as an extra. However, the job won't last long, maybe another week at the most, since we're almost finished here."

Completely surprised by the offer, Megan didn't hesitate. "Why, yes, I'll do that. When do I start?"

"Be there first thing tomorrow morning. And you know the routine. I'll advise wardrobe so they'll be expecting you early, around six, and when you're finished there and at makeup, you should be able to get to the set by eight. You can do this, can't you?"

"No problem, sir. And do I need to bring my own horse?"

Eller paused a moment. "Yes, but I don't know if you'll use it or one of ours. However, it might be good to have it on hand, just in case."

Seeming uneasy and anxious to leave, Eller shook Jim's hand, assuring him once more that his check would arrive soon. Looking at Megan, Eller said, "I'll see you on the set tomorrow by eight, right?"

Without waiting for a response, the director hurried to the store leaving Megan and her dad standing there, trying to catch their breath. Finally, Jim said, "Come on, girl, get in the truck. We've got grocery shopping to do."

Leaving the parking lot and heading toward the new supermarket, Jim asked his daughter, "Are you serious about doing this acting stuff?"

"What do you mean by serious?" Megan knew she didn't have the answer he wanted to hear and stalled for time.

"Well, is this the line of work you want to do?" Jim's tone was becoming more than slightly agitated.

"No, Dad, I don't want to be a movie star. But I do enjoy working with animals and right now I can do this on the set and pick up a few bucks at the same time."

"But didn't he say you were going to do stunt work?"

"Yes, but that means I'll be on horseback."

"Are you sure? Maybe you'll be leaping off of buildings too."

"No, Dad, I don't think I'll be doing that."

"Well, when are you going get a real job?"

By now they'd reached the grocery store's parking lot and Megan wished her dad would hurry up and park, ending this awkward conversation. However, as they walked inside the store, he brought up the subject again.

"It's time, you know, to start looking for a real job."

"I know that, Dad, and I'm working on it."

"Oh?"

"Yes, I've already sent out two resumes."

"Well, very good, I'm glad to hear it!"

Yeah, maybe for you but the movie business is what works for me. With that, she ran over to the frozen desserts and picked out a chocolate ice cream bar to calm her nerves.

Pulling firmly on the reins, Gil brought Geronimo to a stop. "Cut!" the director shouted through his speaker horn. "That's a wrap." Then he added, "Gil, can I talk to you for a minute?"

Hearing this, Gil turned his horse and headed toward the rear of the set. There he found Eller in the director's chair, sitting comfortably as he orchestrated the scenes and camera angles.

Dismounting by the bed of a nearby truck, he tied up his horse and walked over to Eller, but found Angela there too. Judging from the director's facial expression, she'd just said something he didn't want to hear, so Gil felt safe when interrupting. "You wanted to see me?"

"What?" Eller appeared startled. "Oh, yes, Gil. Uh . . . oh! I wanted to ask you for a favor. Do you think you could spend some time helping Megan Wakefield? I just hired her to be Angela's double. She may be new to acting but she does know her way around horses. So, if you could maybe work with her a little this afternoon and show her what she needs to do in tomorrow's shoot,

I'd really appreciate it. We're close to the end here and need to wrap this thing up as quickly as possible. And, if you can keep us from having to re-shoot any more than necessary tomorrow, that would be great. What do you say? Can you do this?"

Both Gil and Angela seemed surprised by the news, and though he appeared pleased, the actress clearly wasn't. "Sure, Paul, I can do that. I'll check the script and see what she needs to know."

"Maybe I can help you, Gil." Angela came around from the side of Eller's chair to stand next to him. "I have a copy of the script back at the Honey Wagon and, if you like, we could go over it together now." Her warm smile, accented by lowered eyelids casting a seductive glance toward Gil, brought an immediate reaction from Eller.

"No need for that," he said, bouncing to his feet and shoving an extra script into Gil's hand. "Here's your own copy, Gil." Turning to face the actress, Eller added, "Besides, I need to talk to you some more before your next scene, and I thought we could do that over at the food tent?"

Gil felt relieved but could tell Angela wasn't. So, thanking Eller for the script, he added, "I'll try to set up a meeting with Megan right away and get her prepared."

"But you just did that the other day, didn't you, Gil?" asked Angela.

"What do you mean?" Gil was puzzled.

"Well, I saw, I mean I heard you trained her to fall from a horse. What happened? Couldn't she do it right?" Angela's voice was filled with sarcasm.

So you were the one out in the woods watching us? Shocked but keeping his voice under control, Gil answered, "Oh, Megan did it right. In fact, she did really well. But not being familiar with what she has to do tomorrow, I'll go over the script, like Paul said, and clue her in on what to expect."

This seemed to upset Angela even more and, turning abruptly, she began to walk away, but not before telling Eller, "I'll meet you at the catering tent in half an hour. Don't be late."

As he watched her leave, Gil asked, "What's with her?"

Eller responded with a shrug. "Can't say, really. But thanks for doing this, Gil." And the director began to follow Angela but seemed in no hurry to catch up.

Gil untied his horse, mounted, and rode to the edge of the set. There, Geronimo took off at a fairly brisk pace and the warm air rushing across his body was thoroughly exhilarating, just what Gil needed to remove all those tense feelings.

Megan, home from town and having eaten lunch, hid in her room and, for her folks' benefit, was pretending to send out another resume. So when Gil called and asked if they could meet in an hour or so at the back pasture to rehearse her scene for the next day, she had been pleased. But after hanging up and telling her parents that she was about to leave and why, she could see that her dad clearly wasn't happy.

"You mean you aren't going to work this afternoon on finding a job?"

"I can't right now. I don't have time," Megan replied, inching her way out of the room. She wanted to go change into something a little more eye-catching and was thankful when her father didn't pursue the argument any further.

It took about twenty minutes to get herself and her horse ready for the trip. At Gil's request, she was to come on horseback. Since the animal wasn't required to fall, and would just be ridden alongside the cattle, Gil didn't think a specially trained horse was necessary.

The script called for the female star or, in this case, her double, to herd a large group of cows across the pasture and down toward the river. Megan remembered hearing her dad say something earlier to her mom about this scene. Since it was to be shot on land not originally included in the movie company's contract, they had cleared it with Jim first.

Megan, arriving at the pasture, found Gil already there waiting and, as he greeted her, she caught a glimpse of personal satisfaction in his smile. However, Gil's manner then became all business.

Megan had herded a lot of cows in her lifetime but she'd never had to worry about camera angles and such, so she listened intently as Gil explained the ins and outs of this venture. Being a quick study, it wasn't long before Megan felt she had it down pat so Gil suggested that Megan get back on her horse and practice what he had just described.

Holding an imaginary camera, he ran alongside and pretended to be filming her actions as she mounted her horse, prompting it to walk. Megan soon discovered this was a little more complicated than she'd first thought. But after several tries and incorporating Gil's suggestions, she finally felt comfortable with the process.

The big surprise came later, after the training session. Megan, her foot in the stirrup, was preparing to head for home when Gil asked, "How about dinner tonight?"

Removing her foot from the stirrup, Megan turned. "What did you say?"

"I asked if you'd like to have dinner with me tonight?" Gil was wearing a neutral expression, as if her positive or negative answer would have no effect on him.

"Where, in town?" she asked, causing Gil to laugh.

"Why? Does your answer depend on the location?"

"No, of course it doesn't." Megan felt really asinine, something she'd been experiencing a lot lately. "What I meant to say is, yes, I'll have dinner with you and where will we be eating?"

Gil didn't answer. Instead he kept looking at her. Finally, he asked, "How about at my RV?"

Really caught off guard, Megan stammered, "Your RV?"

"Yeah, I picked up a large order of barbeque from

Pete's Place in town yesterday and have plenty left. I thought maybe we could just finish it up at my place and then call it an early night since we both have to be on the set at dawn tomorrow."

Though surprised by his invitation, Megan quickly accepted. Gil said he'd pick her up at six, if that was okay, and she agreed. And, after mounting, each galloped off, once more, in opposite directions.

As promised, Gil arrived promptly at six to pick her up. After a quick good-bye to her parents, and with no mention of their destination, they drove back to his place with little or no conversation. But Megan didn't find the silence uncomfortable. Her uneasiness began when they arrived at the camp and she saw several people staring at them as they entered his RV together.

What are they thinking? Megan wondered, though she already had a good idea. Earlier, when telling her mom and dad about this dinner date, she'd been careful to avoid mentioning its location. Since she was twenty-one, Megan knew her parents were trying to let go, to allow her, as an adult, to make decisions. They still offered parental advice, though, and she figured this would be one of those times.

Megan trusted Gil completely, but nagging worries about what others might think went on even after they were inside the trailer and up until the barbeque was heated and ready to eat. But then her hungry stomach took over, halting these insecure feelings, and the evening turned out to be a delightful experience, with tasty food and all. While they ate, Gil gave her some insight on the movie and animal business.

"Thanks, Gil," she told him after he finished. "This is all so new to me and it can get confusing at times."

"Believe me; I know what you're saying. It's taken me the past five years or so to figure this much out."

Finishing the meal, and ignoring Gil's objections, Megan went to the sink and began washing the few dinner dishes while he turned on the CD player. Before long, she heard Willie Nelson singing one of his popular songs. *Strange, Gil's choice of music is the same as mine.*

With the dishes finished, Megan went to the RV's living room and sat down on the built-in sofa. Quickly joining her, Gil asked, "How was the barbeque?"

"Really good, but of course I've always thought that Pete's Place made the very best, in this part of Texas, at least." She was becoming very much aware of Gil's nearness and could feel warm, strong emotions beginning to surface. As they sat listening to Willie sing another song, and though Megan automatically moved a few inches further away from him, she could still feel the desire growing, giving the atmosphere a heightened charge of anticipation.

Gil put his arm around her shoulders and Megan truly felt safe and special. She realized the feelings had been there since they first met. So when he leaned over to kiss her, Megan eagerly responded.

He pressed his mouth against hers and sensing his

need, Megan raised her hands and gently placed one on either side of his face, and parted her lips.

Minutes later, when the kiss ended, Megan remained close and putting her head on his shoulder, sighed. At that moment, Gil knew he should back off, resist the clawing heat radiating from his body, but it was too late. There she was, in his arms, her body warm and lush. So he pulled her even closer, inhaling her scent, and seeking her lips.

He'd had his share of women in the past, ones who had given him deep, skillful kisses and intimate moments. But those past experiences could never measure up to Megan's sweet and sincere kisses. He knew that emotionally she had opened herself to him, without pretending or using any well-practiced ploys.

Most men would have taken full advantage of the way she was responding and, though his feelings urged him to go further, he resisted the growing heat of temptation and backed off. Instead, he quietly held her in his arms as they sat there listening to another Willie Nelson song.

Chapter Eight

Even though it was still early, Megan was ready to go in a silver shirt, black jeans and boots, a carbon copy of what Angela would be wearing. Megan went to retrieve her horse from the base camp's corral, knowing that she would need it that day in the scene Eller was planning to shoot.

When she first got there, it had been dark, but now the sun was shining, and her journey through the pasture to the spot where filming would take place was most pleasant. Mixed feelings of nervousness and excitement continued to linger, but that was all right, despite what her father might think. Megan believed this entire experience was worth the anxiety. After all, not only was she meeting famous and interesting people, but at the same time she was working with animals and getting paid for it. What more could she ask?

Reining her horse up beside a temporary holding pen containing cows to be used in the shoot, Megan dismounted. She saw Eller a short distance away talking to the camera crew. Also, Gil was out there on horseback, riding along with three other men whom she assumed to be wranglers. As she and the cattle were being filmed, those four would be the ones actually doing the work, but out of camera range.

A chauffeured vehicle drove up just then and a few of the people in the area, seeing that Angela had arrived, rushed forward to greet the star. While exiting her car, and in spite of the approaching group, Angela spotted Megan immediately and gave a familiar look of dislike.

So Megan took her horse to a nearby tree and, after securing it, went over where Eller was sitting and telling people what to do and how to do it. Megan guessed that the director was a born organizer, a person who loved being in control of everything and everyone. But when he looked up and saw Megan, his manner altered, mellowing somewhat. Though he didn't wave or call out, it wasn't too long before he got up and walked over to her.

"So glad you made it, Megan. I see you've already been to wardrobe and makeup. That's good; we're just about to start shooting. First, we'll do some close-ups of Angela, and then we'll film you in action. So please, don't go anywhere or leave the area." And, seeing Angela walking in their direction, Eller reached out to give Megan a warm, embrace, making sure that the actress was watching. After that, he hurried back to his director's chair.

Megan knew she was nothing more than a pawn. Eller was using her to try and make his star jealous. His friendly gestures toward Megan and invitations were nothing more than a way to try and claim Angela's attention. Was it working? Megan didn't have a clue. But, from the star's strange actions, Megan was beginning to think that Angela was more jealous of the relationship she had with Gil. And, was Gil aware of this? Megan didn't know since they had never discussed it. Or could he just be using her to make the actress jealous? *No way,* Megan thought, as she remembered the previous night in his RV. In fact, Megan would swear that by the end of their evening Gil was thinking of only one woman, and it wasn't Angela.

These thoughts must have been magnetic because suddenly Gil was there at her side. Though still atop his horse, he gave her one of his warm, masculine, devil-may-care smiles that she found so appealing. "How's it going, Megan?"

"Just great," she replied, with a grin. "But I haven't had to do anything yet so who knows how I'll feel by the time it's all over."

"Probably the same, just great," he said with encouragement. "That is, if you do as well today as you did yesterday." Suddenly he stopped, embarrassed. "I mean, how well you did with the horse out in the pasture yesterday afternoon." Megan realized that Gil, too, was recalling their evening together the previous night.

Trying to mask his nervousness, Gil asked, "You did bring your horse, didn't you?"

"Of course, it's tied to that tree over there." Both looked toward the wooded area and, to their surprise, saw Angela petting Megan's horse.

"That's strange," Gil muttered. "I've never seen her touch or come in contact with any animal unless the script required it."

Megan didn't reply but watched closely as the woman turned away from the horse and walked over toward Eller. Since the director was preparing to shoot the last of Angela's close-ups, Megan figured it wouldn't be long before she herself would be in front of the cameras.

The morning sun was high in the heavens, creating an intense natural light and making the entire task much easier to film.

Gil, with help from the other wranglers, began lining up the cows, walking them slowly across the pasture until three of the longhorns, with minds of their own, decided to go their own way. It took the men almost ten minutes to convince the beasts to cooperate but after that all went well.

With cameras in place, the cattle ready, Gil sat quietly atop his horse and watched Angela, after she said good-bye to Eller, walk to her car and the waiting chauffeur. He saw Megan go over, untie her horse and walk it back to where Eller sat. Gil's thoughts, as he watched her do this, had nothing to do with filmmaking. Instead he kept remembering the night before in his RV. And he knew that if he was a gentleman, he wouldn't be having these kinds of thoughts, but still he couldn't stop them. Or, maybe, didn't want to.

Suddenly, Geronimo reared up to avoid being hit by a steer that had broken away from the group and Gil's attention was yanked back to the present. It was one of the three that had given them trouble earlier and Gil, as head wrangler, immediately took charge. Pulling on the reins, he brought Geronimo under control and headed to the disruptive longhorn, forcing it back into the herd.

When all was again quiet, Eller's voice, magnified by the handheld bullhorn, ordered Megan to mount up and begin her ride alongside the moving cattle. Gil watched as she slid her foot into the stirrup and swung up into the saddle. But, just then, her horse's movements told him things weren't as they should be and Megan was in trouble. He knew she had worked with horses most of her life and was experienced. But if what he thought was about to occur, she was in serious trouble.

Instinctively, he turned and urged Geronimo into action but before he could reach Megan, Gil saw exactly what he had feared begin to unfold. First, her horse reared up on its hind legs, then began to run, jump, and buck. Soon the animal altered its pace and, leaning its head down toward the ground, kicked up its hind legs. Not bothering to analyze the reason for all of this, Gil simply charged forward, trying to grab the reins and bring the horse to a stop.

But the animal leaped in the opposite direction and his first attempt failed. Gil, now close enough to get a good view of Megan, saw that she was trying without success to control the animal as it reared up again. Her right foot slipped from the stirrup causing Megan to lose her balance. Instinctively, she reached for the saddle horn as the animal jumped in the opposite direction, toward Gil, and this time he was able to grab the leather straps. But before he could bring the animal to a complete stop, Megan fell off.

Thanks to some quick thinking, Gil pulled firmly, turning his horse away from Megan on the ground, preventing any further damage. And, to his surprise, all the commotion ceased. The horse was no longer jumping and kicking, but just standing there, breathing heavily. *That's strange,* Gil thought.

Eller and several others had started toward them and, in the distance, Gil saw Angela standing at the open door of her van watching. But then she closed the door and began walking back toward them. Gil figured the actress must have waited around to watch this, but he wondered how she knew in advance that something was going to happen.

Jumping down from Geronimo, Gil ran over to Megan on the ground. Gathering her in his arms, he saw she was still short of breath from the fall and had blood on her forehead, but she seemed to be okay and there didn't appear to be anything broken. Of course, it would take x-rays to accurately confirm this.

"Oh," she moaned.

Gil held her closely and whispered, "It's all right. You're all right now. You're safe." Just then he felt a hand on his shoulder. It was Bob, one of the wranglers.

"How is she?" he asked.

"I can't tell for sure, but I think she's okay. Of course, there'll be a few bruises."

"What's that on her forehead?" Bob asked.

"Looks like a small cut, but not very deep. I don't think it'll need stitches and probably will heal if it's taped up for a while."

"What happened?" Megan asked, her voice weak. "What's wrong with my horse? Why did it act like that?"

"I don't know yet but I'm going to find out." Just then, Gil caught a glimpse of Angela standing at the far side of the corral and she seemed upset at seeing the girl in this condition. *Or maybe it isn't that. Maybe it's because I'm holding Megan in my arms.* But, her injuries quickly reclaimed his attention. "We need to get you to the hospital."

"Oh no, I'm sore but nothing's broken. Here, help me up." She tried to break away from his grip.

"Not just yet," Gil said, worried.

But Megan was insistent. "Help me up, now!" she demanded, while trying to get on her feet.

Then, Eller appeared. "Gil! Let her go! Megan, are you okay? I'm calling EMS." It was quite apparent that Eller was worried about Megan, or maybe that the shoot would have to be put on hold.

However, Megan responded quickly. "No, Paul, that isn't necessary. But, I would like to go home now."

Gil and Bob helped her up onto her feet. Still a little shaky, Megan was holding onto Gil's arm. Seeing this, Eller relaxed and seemed a little more comfortable with the entire situation.

"Sure. Sure. I'll have one of the drivers take you home, Megan, and Gil will bring your horse."

With a helping hand under each arm, Megan was escorted to the waiting van. Gil noticed she appeared to be okay, nothing broken, although her body had taken quite a beating and pain was causing her to flinch occasionally.

He watched the van drive off then went to check on Megan's horse. The animal was standing quietly near the cow pen; all the kicking and bucking had stopped. "Hey," said Eller, coming up behind him. "You don't mind taking this horse back to Megan's now, do you, Gil? It's caused enough trouble for one day."

"No, Paul, not at all. But shouldn't I help out here on the set first?"

"Well, Megan isn't available so we can't film that segment today. And I'm sure the wranglers can re-pen the cows without your help." Gil thought he detected some antagonism coming from the man, something that seemed to be happening a lot lately.

"Okay then," Gil said, "I'll just ride my horse and lead Megan's home." Eller, with a nod of approval, walked away.

The trip to Wakefield's house was uneventful and, before announcing his presence, Gil led the animal into one of the corrals. It was while removing the saddle that he found the answer to the horse's earlier outburst. Something sharp jabbed into his hand and, looking closer at the underside of the saddle blanket, Gil found a large, prickly thorn. It was positioned in such a way that when someone sat down, their weight would push the sharply pointed vegetation into the horse's flesh, causing severe pain. Gil knew, however, that if it had been there when Megan first saddled her horse, she would have discovered the thorn immediately. Consequently, someone else had intentionally put it under the blanket, someone who planned to cause the very problems that occurred. *But why? Who could possibly want to hurt Megan?*

Chapter Nine

Early the next day, and against her dad's wishes, Megan was back on the set. Yes, she was sore, but no, it wasn't bad enough to keep her from saddling her horse and riding over to the base camp. Once there, the lady in wardrobe exchanged Megan's tattered costume, damaged during the accident, for an identical one. The makeup artist miraculously made the bruises and cut on her forehead disappear.

Megan thought that Eller, who had called the previous evening, sounded quite relieved upon hearing that she planned to return to work right away, and he had quickly explained what needed to be done at wardrobe and makeup. Megan had no problem with this, but her parents weren't at all pleased. The previous day, as they watched the van driver help their daughter limp up the steps and into the house, Megan's mom and dad panicked. It became even worse as Megan described what had happened. But after finally convincing them that she didn't need to go to the hospital, Megan saw her dad's worry turn to anger.

"I made a terrible mistake letting them on my property," he said as Megan and Naomi tried to remain calm.

"Jim, it wasn't anyone's fault; these things just happen," Naomi tried to explain as her husband continued to rant and rave.

And, her dad had been less than civil when Gil showed up at the back door, to let them know he had brought Megan's horse home. Jim's replies to the young man's inquiry about Megan's well-being were curt and abrupt. In fact, he practically slammed the door in Gil's face.

Later, when Megan informed her parents that she planned to go back to work the following day, her dad became furious. By now, though, Megan realized that a lot of his anger was due to money problems and not receiving the checks. His daughter being injured was merely the last straw.

Regardless, Megan stood her ground. She found this work exciting and still wanted to perform and appear in the movie. Also, it would provide a chance to see Gil, once again.

But as she rode into the back pasture and onto the set, Gil wasn't visible. She did locate Eller and headed in his direction, stopping her horse a short distance from where he and Angela stood. As always, Eller was impeccably groomed, wearing his tobacco-brown silk sports coat over a white dress shirt and cream-colored trousers. Angela was attired in her costume, with makeup applied, ready for her next shoot scheduled right after Megan's.

It didn't take Megan long to figure out that the two were having a heated argument and, although she wasn't that close, Megan thought she heard Angela yell that she wanted a different double. That's when the director looked up and saw Megan. His face broke into an automatic smile and, without another word to his star, hurried over to Megan who was still atop her horse.

"Oh my goodness, it's so good to see you here, my dear. How are you feeling?" Inspecting her more closely he went on to say, "They did a terrific job in makeup and covered up any signs of injury from your fall."

Eller rattled on some more as he helped Megan down from her horse and when she was safely on the ground, made no attempt to remove his arm that lay across her shoulders. But she wasn't fooled, especially, when she saw him cast a sly glance over at his star. *He's just trying again to make Angela jealous.*

Slightly annoyed with all of this adolescent game playing, she removed herself from his grasp and, interrupting whatever he was trying to say, Megan asked, "Are you going to film my part today?"

"Oh, yes," said the director. "In fact, we need to get started." Eller moved around so that he, and not Megan, faced Angela, apparently in an attempt to keep Angela unaware of Megan's displeasure.

But Angela couldn't care less about that. Instead, her annoyance seemed to come from being left alone in the background. So, to change this, she marched over to where the two stood and began stating her demands.

"I need Gil, right now, to come help me with my next horse scene," she insisted.

Seemingly right on cue, Gil rode up. Needless to say, a deep frown appeared on the director's face. Apparently, this wasn't part of his plan.

To make matters even worse, Gil dismounted and went directly over to Megan, totally ignoring Eller and Angela. "I'm surprised to see you here today. How are you feeling?"

"A little sore, but other than that, okay." Feeling waves of tension coming from the other two, Megan stopped talking and Angela stepped in and took over.

Grabbing Gil by the arm, she began to lead him off in the opposite direction. "I'm so glad you're here," she cooed. "I need you to show me a few things before my next scene. You can do that now, can't you?" As an afterthought and with a syrupy smile, she added, "Pretty please?"

"Well, I don't know," Gil answered, turning to look at Eller. "Don't you need me here, Paul, to help with the cows and Megan?"

Megan saw that both the director and star were far from happy. *What a way to begin my career as an actress,* she thought. So, feeling she had little or nothing to lose, Megan tossed her own two-cents-worth into the mix.

"May I make a suggestion? I think, having read the script, that I can handle it. I've worked with cows most of my life and don't believe I'll have any trouble. So, Paul, go ahead and have Gil help Angela, and we'll go and get this scene on film."

Not knowing what to say, and definitely not pleased, Eller agreed. Angela, on the other hand, was ecstatic and immediately led a thoroughly confused Gil, along with his horse, off in the opposite direction.

Though Gil tried to keep things strictly professional, this wasn't Angela's agenda and she made it a point, as often as possible, to get as physically close to him as possible. One time she feigned a stumble, causing her to land in his arms, her face just inches away from his. Another time, Angela asked him to feel along the inside of her waistband to see if he could find the sticker she thought was caught in there. He did this as carefully and cautiously as possible, while she seized the opportunity to run her fingers through his hair and down the side of his face. Finally, Gil helped her up onto the horse and, for a short while, kept her at a comfortable distance.

Earlier, though, when she had mentioned the sticker, his mind had gone back to the one he had found under Megan's saddle blanket. Gil had wanted to tell Wakefield about it the night before, but Jim, having slammed the door in his face, didn't give him the chance.

He planned to mention it to Eller that morning. But that plan was thwarted, as well, when Angela sidetracked him.

Now, with Angela on her horse and doing as he had instructed, Gil glanced over where they were filming and was pleased to see Megan performing so well. He noticed, though, that Eller was spending less time directing Megan and more time watching Angela. The actress, however, was completely disinterested in what Eller or anyone else was doing and kept trying to get closer and create a compromising situation with him.

Finally, in desperation, Gil said, "I think you've got this down pat, Angela. You shouldn't have any problems when the camera rolls."

"And that's because of all your wonderful help." Getting down from her horse, Angela walked over to Gil. "I couldn't have done it without you and I think I need to buy you dinner tonight as a way of showing my gratitude. What do you think? How about we go and get some of Pete's barbeque?"

Gil didn't know what to say. He certainly didn't want to go, but she was the movie's leading lady so how could he politely refuse? However, Eller appeared just then and saved him from having to answer. The director ignored Gil and went straight over to Angela. "I need to talk to you, right away," he said. But, her reply, "Sure, go ahead," wasn't the response he was looking for.

"No. Not here. Come and walk with me."

Feeling dismissed by both, a thankful Gil uttered his unreturned good-byes and, climbing up into the saddle, he and Geronimo started off in the opposite direction. But then Angela called out, "What about tonight, Gil?"

However, pretending he hadn't heard her, Gil again ducked his obligation of having to answer.

The scene had gone well and Megan was extremely pleased, confident that she had done the job professionally. And because the wranglers had done such a good job of keeping the animals from causing any trouble, the cattle had played their parts well too. And, while Eller had yelled "Cut" from time to time to issue more instructions, Megan felt his attention had not really been on the shoot. Often she caught him looking over at the pasture area where Gil was helping Angela, and as soon as he yelled "That's a wrap," Eller had jumped from his chair to head in that direction.

Bob, one of the wranglers, came over to ask how she was feeling and interrupted her thoughts. "A little sore, but not too bad." In an effort to change the subject, Megan asked, "How do you think it went today?"

"Seemed okay to me, but what do I know? From the way Eller acted, though, I think he was satisfied." Then, Bob added, "Maybe we can work together again sometime."

"Maybe, and thanks for your help."

"No problem." Giving Megan a warm smile, Bob headed off to help the other wranglers pen up the cows.

Now alone, Megan leaned up against the side of a large, parked semi-trailer that had been used to haul movie props. While trying to decide what to do next, she heard voices coming from the other side of the vehicle and the extremely vocal discussion immediately caught her attention.

"Fire Gil? Why would you want to do that?" a woman's voice said. Though she couldn't see anyone, it sounded like Angela.

"Because I think it's his fault that Megan's horse acted up yesterday. I don't know exactly what, but he did something wrong, something that made the animal react like that." This voice she did recognize as Eller's.

"Oh, you're being ridiculous. Anyway, who would you hire in his place?" The actress sounded upset.

"I don't know. We have several possible replacements; one being Megan."

"What? You want to replace Gil with that dimwitted little witch? I know the only reason you hired her as my double in the first place was to try and appease her dad for the late checks."

"Maybe," said Eller, "maybe not."

Is that why he hired me? Megan wondered, wishing she hadn't heard any of this. Now angry, all she wanted to do was get on her horse and ride away. But thinking more about it, part of her couldn't help but be glad he had hired her, whatever the reason. So she remained right where she was and continued to eavesdrop.

Megan heard Angela say, "Well, if you do that, hire her and fire Gil, you can also look for someone to take my place because I'll quit!"

"You can't do that," Eller said smugly.

"Just watch me!" Angela retorted.

"Okay then, go ahead and quit if you want to. I'll just have Megan fill in for you. There are only three small scenes left before we wrap up this picture. And you do know that if you don't show up, your contract becomes null and void."

"That's a lot of bull. And I do quit, so there! But, if you touch my contract, I'll take you to court so fast—"

"Just watch me!" Eller interrupted her.

It sounded to Megan as though one of them had walked away. Not caring who was watching, Megan ran over, got on her horse, and left as quickly as she could. She felt life was becoming far too complicated.

During the ride home, Megan kept hoping that her dad wouldn't be there. She just wanted to go to her room, close the door, and not have to talk to anyone. Megan knew her mother would be okay with this, but not her dad. However, as she got closer to the house, the first thing she noticed was her father's truck in the driveway and his horse in the corral.

It grew worse. Entering through the back door, she found both parents in the kitchen; Jim was talking loudly as her mother listened. And, having seen her arrive, there was no escape. Bubba came running over to greet her, apparently upset by her dad's yelling.

"I don't know why I ever got into this mess. I just hope I'm never tempted to do it again," said her dad.

"Now, Jim, it isn't that bad. I realize they're late in paying you, but Mr. Eller said that you'll have a check by next Monday. But what happened to Megan was an accident, and thankfully not that serious." She was doing all she could to pacify her husband but it wasn't working. So, attempting to change the subject, Naomi acknowledged her daughter's arrival. "Hi there, girl, how was your day?"

"It was fine, Mom. I think I did okay." Megan was careful not to mention what she had overheard or witnessed on the set.

"Well, you won't be doing this anymore," her dad declared angrily. "I'm going to pull the plug. I'm calling my lawyer first thing Monday morning and telling him to cancel the contract because of non-payment and I'll have those people off my ranch by sundown."

"Daddy, you can't do that!" Megan exclaimed. She really didn't want the movie to be finished. And, even more than that, if her dad should stop the filming and they went somewhere else, would she ever see Gil again?

"Yes, I can. And I will!" With that said Jim left the kitchen and went outside to the corral.

"Mom, don't let him do this." Megan was beginning to panic. "Please talk to him."

"Oh, I can talk to him all right but I'm not sure he'll

listen. First, let him cool down a bit and then we'll see what can be done."

"Do you think you can stop him?" Megan suddenly realized she had aroused her mother's curiosity.

"Why do you care so much?"

"Oh, I don't know. It's just that they're almost finished and I'd hate for them to have to start all over." She was careful not to mention her fear of never seeing Gil again, though she felt her mother might just understand.

And then, who should show up at the back door but Gil. After the three exchanged greetings, Megan took him into the living room while Naomi went out to the barn to talk to Jim some more. "How did the shoot go today? Did you have any problems?" Gil asked, as they sat down on the sofa.

"No. The shoot went fine. I just hope it isn't their last one."

"Why? What do you mean? They still have two or three more scenes to finish and then several days of wrapping up."

"Well, just before you arrived, my dad was carrying on about canceling their contract for lack of payment."

"Lack of payment? You mean he hasn't been paid yet?"

"Oh yes, he was getting a check regularly up until four weeks ago. Eller told him the problem was due to a computer error and, come Monday, he'd be paid in full. But Dad doesn't believe it."

"Well then it's a good thing I've got that gig to do tomorrow," said Gil, nervously running a hand through his hair.

"You mean you're doing something else beside the movie?"

"I'm not scheduled to be on the set this weekend, so I lucked out and was offered another job providing animals for a TV commercial in Austin. It'll only take one day, but will sure help my empty bank account."

"Providing animals? That sounds interesting. What kind of animals?"

"They want a mule, a pig, and six chickens."

"And you can find all of them in time?"

Gil smiled. "I already have them. Like I told you, I've been accumulating livestock for a while now, so I have the mule and pig. Chickens, I can borrow from a guy I know."

"Oh yes, I remember now. These are some of the animals you keep at your friend's ranch." Her interest was genuine and the fact that she could remember Gil telling her all this seemed to please him too. "That's great, Gil, and I'm impressed that you can combine an additional business in with acting. It must be a great way to make a living."

Gil didn't answer. Instead, he sat there looking at her, a thoughtful expression on his face. Then he asked, "Would you like to go with me tomorrow, Megan, into Austin and see all this firsthand, or do you have something else on your agenda?"

"Really, could I?" she felt herself getting excited.

"Yes, I'd like that and no, I don't have anything else on my schedule."

"Good. I'll pick you up in the morning at six. Or is that too early?"

"No, no, that'll be fine. And thanks for inviting me."

As he leaned toward her, she followed his lead and soon their lips touched and their arms automatically encircled one another. *More! More!* her mind screamed, just as they heard the back door open and close. Megan, knowing at least one of her parents had returned, pulled away from Gil's embrace, squelching the moment.

"Megan, honey," her mother called out from the kitchen. Upon entering the living room, Naomi said, "Oh, there you are."

Realizing that her mother was looking at them strangely, Megan nervously said, "Guess what, Mom? Gil's invited me to go with him to Austin tomorrow. He's working as head wrangler for a company filming a commercial there and is bringing his own animals. Isn't that great?"

"Why, yes, it is. I didn't know you had animals, Gil. Do you have your own ranch too?"

"No, not yet, but hopefully one day I will. I don't have that many and, right now, my friend's dad is letting them stay on his ranch. But I keep accumulating more and hope one day I can turn all this into a full-time business. You know, have them available and on call when needed. Believe it or not, there's a demand and people often want to rent animals for various reasons. The hard part is spreading the word and trying to make connections with the right people."

Gil rose from the couch, followed by Megan. She knew he was preparing to leave and really didn't want him to go. *I'll be spending all day tomorrow with him,* she thought, and smiled as she walked him to the door and politely said good-bye.

Chapter Ten

"More coffee?" the waiter asked, having stopped at their table with a steaming pot in his hands.

"I don't care for anymore, thanks," said Megan.

"How about you, sir?"

"No thanks. I've had plenty," Gil said.

As the waiter moved on, Megan reached out and placed her hand on top of Gil's. "Thanks so much for inviting me along today. It was all so interesting and even fun. I think your business of supplying animals is fascinating. It's something I know I'd enjoy doing."

"The pleasure's all mine, Megan. And besides, your quick reaction was great when that chicken tried to escape and flew right at the cameraman." Both laughed as they recalled the incident.

"No problem. In fact, like I said, I enjoy working

with animals and would like to do it as a profession. But my dad doesn't quite see things the same way. And besides, I really wouldn't know where to start."

Gil looked at Megan, a thoughtful expression on his face. "Well then, how about joining me again on Thursday? It just so happens that while I was on the set today, Joe Williams, who is also in the film business, came up and asked if I could provide three horses for a commercial. I told him I could and, Megan, if you could help again, that would be great."

"What about Eller's movie? Don't you have to be there on Thursday too?"

"No. I should be finished by then. Paul said Tuesday would be my last day."

Then Megan remembered the conversation she had overheard the day before between the director and Angela but she knew she couldn't just come right out and tell Gil that Eller planned to fire him and put her in his place.

"How about it, Megan, do you want to help me out on Thursday?"

Megan couldn't refuse his request. In the first place, it was work she liked doing and second, it meant spending another entire day with Gil. She had enjoyed this day so much doing the TV commercial, and was pleased to discover they worked well as a team. There had been no arguments or disagreements. He hadn't been bossy, nor had she been stubborn. Besides, Megan enjoyed being around the animals, and here he was offering her another opportunity to do just that.

"Sure Gil, if they don't need me on the set, I'll be glad to come along and help you. Just let me know when and where." Her answer seemed to please him.

With dinner over, they gathered their belongings, left the restaurant, and walked over to Gil's truck and the attached trailer containing the mule, pig, and six chickens. Megan was sure that by this time, the animals were ready to go home, eat something, and bed down for the night.

It was a good hour's drive back to her father's ranch in Wayside but since it was only eight o'clock both she and Gil seemed to be enjoying the ride home. Earlier, he mentioned how impressed he was with the way she had handled the animals. And now, sitting there next to him in the cab of his truck, Megan felt a sense of satisfaction as well as those strong warm, romantic sensations she'd been experiencing lately.

When they finally pulled up in front of her house, Gil turned off the engine but didn't attempt to move or open the door. This came as no surprise nor did it upset Megan. In fact, it pleased her very much. Especially when Gil moved closer. Within seconds Megan was in his arms, her lips enveloped by his. She felt warm desire rush through her, and her body tremble.

In time, Gil withdrew his lips. Looking into his eyes, she could see his needs were much like those of her own. Although he tried to appear calm and in control, his jaw tightened and she knew that he desired and wanted her too. "I'm going to miss you," Gil said.

"What do you mean, miss me? We'll be seeing each other next week, won't we?"

"Yes, we will. But then, I'll be leaving this area for a while."

"Leaving? Where are you going? What are you going to do?" She could hear the distress in her voice.

"George Neil, another guy I was talking to today, just before we left the set in Austin, is directing a new movie that'll begin filming soon in Little Rock. He wants me as a stunt double and also as head wrangler; the same things I'm doing for Eller."

"Little Rock? But that's so far away. How long will you be gone?"

"Four, maybe five or six months," he answered. This sounded like a lifetime to Megan. Suddenly, the passion, which only moments earlier had surged through her body, withered and evaporated. He was going to leave her and all this would be gone.

"But you can't do that." Shocked, Megan couldn't believe she had just said that and was actually pleading for him to stay.

Gil placed his lips, once again, lightly upon hers, ending Megan's protests. But this slow, sweet kiss, one that seemed to squelch her will power and turn her bones to jelly, came to an abrupt halt when the truck began to shake and loud noises erupted from the attached trailer. Then as suddenly as it had started it stopped.

Removing his arm from her shoulders, Gil jumped

out of the cab and ran to the rear of the truck with Megan close behind. Upon reaching the back of the trailer, the shaking and jerking started up again. Something was loose and running around inside.

Gil tried to look through the small barred window, but it was dark and he couldn't see anything. So he unlocked the door to the trailer. Just as Megan was about to warn him to be careful, she saw the door shoved open, pushed from his grasp, and the pig jump out, knocking Gil to the ground. Megan tried to help him but Gil called out, "Hurry, close the trailer door before the mule escapes too." Megan stood up to do it but while looking inside she found the mule still attached to a pole.

"It's okay, Gil, the mule's tied up, but what are we going to do about the pig?" Her watch read ten-thirty and, of course, it was much too dark to find anything. They would have to wait until the sun came up. Gil should have been better prepared and more careful when he opened that door.

"I'll just have to come back in the morning to look for her. Hopefully, it won't take too long to find that mindless pig and, if you don't mind, I'll bring Geronimo along."

"From what I saw, it wasn't the pig that was brainless and unlocked the door so carelessly."

Gil seemed surprised at Megan's remark and, though she was smiling, he didn't think it was very funny. And now Megan wished that she'd kept her mouth shut. Especially when he didn't invite her back into the cab of his truck but, instead, took her arm and started to lead her toward the house.

"Thanks for your help today, Megan," he said when they arrived at the porch. "I'll come back early tomorrow to look for the pig and, no doubt, I'll see you then. 'Bye." Without a farewell kiss or any other romantic overture, Gil turned and headed back toward his truck leaving Megan standing there, mouth gaping, feeling a little guilty, and thinking, *Surely, I didn't offend him that much, did I*?

The following morning, and despite the broad assortment of feelings that had allowed her only meager periods of sleep, Megan attacked a stack of pancakes on the plate in front of her with enthusiasm. Her mother had even supplied a cup of hot chocolate to go with breakfast. Knowing this delectable meal would never appear in anyone's meticulous diet plan didn't deter Megan's appetite. Also, listening to her dad's usual speech wasn't a problem. Anything to get her mind off the previous evening and those things she didn't want to think about.

"Any word on your job applications?" he asked.

"Not yet, Dad, but I hope to hear something soon. I've just been so tied up lately, working in the movie and then with those animals yesterday, I just haven't had time to follow up on it."

"Oh, speaking of animals, when I went out to feed

the horses in the corral this morning, I found a pig chewing on a bale of hay. It didn't even run off when it saw me, so I was able to get a rope around its neck and take it over to the goat's old pen. I'm assuming this is Gil's pig, the one that ran off last night."

Though happy to hear the pig was found, it also brought back thoughts of Gil and the fact that he planned to leave and be gone for several months. *How can he just go off like that and leave me? Sure, it's a job and he has to work, but I'll miss him so much. Do I expect him to give up his work for me? Of course not! But maybe he could try and find something closer. Or will he just go somewhere else, maybe even further away, when the Little Rock shoot is over? And why all this now, just when I thought something was beginning to happen between us, something that might last forever?*

Unable to control these thoughts, Megan started to believe she'd been kidding herself all along and was just another babe Gil put the make on. She had to admit, though, it had almost worked. These thoughts killed her appetite and Megan pushed away her plate, still half full of pancakes.

"Aren't you going to finish that?" her dad asked, as Naomi, at the stove making more pancakes, turned to look.

"No, I'm full," said Megan. "In fact, I think I'll go to my room and get started right away on those job applications." And she planned to do just that! No more daydreaming over some guy. No more looking for love in all the wrong places. Megan would take control and begin creating a real and sensible future for herself, one that involved the world of business. No more pretending that she could find a job working with animals, or make a living in the movie industry, or do all this with someone she was beginning to think she'd come to love, someone who apparently didn't feel the same way about her. Forcing a smile for her parents' benefit, Megan headed to the sanctity of her own room, accompanied by Bubba.

Closing the door, she lay on her bed and pulled a pillow over her face, attempting to escape from the outside world. Meanwhile, Bubba lay quietly on the floor beside her, but this lasted only seconds. In spite of the pillow, she heard a vehicle drive up outside, a door slam, and then the doorbell rang. Getting up, she went over to her bedroom window, and saw out front exactly what she didn't want to see—Gil's truck and trailer.

She opened her window slightly, and while she couldn't see the front door or hear what was being said, she recognized the muffled voices as those belonging to Gil and her dad. Should she go to the door too? Even though she really wanted to, Megan decided to stay put and pretend Gil was nothing in her life and that his being there, so close, didn't matter at all.

However, unable to stop herself, Megan quietly opened her door and slipped across the hall into her parents' bedroom. There, she watched from the window as her dad led Gil to his pig, penned up out back.

Peering through the sheer curtains, Megan thought she saw Gil glance up at the house, as if looking for her. *No, he's not. He doesn't even care. Why, he probably has a date with Angela when he gets finished here, and why not? After all, she is a glamorous movie star who definitely seems to have the hots for him.*

But these unsettling thoughts were interrupted when Megan heard the phone ring; a well-timed blessing. Not wanting to be caught in her parent's room watching Gil, she ran back across the hall with Bubba following. She got to her room just as her mother called for her, that the phone was for her. *Who can that be?* Wasting no time, Megan went to the kitchen and picked up the receiver.

"Hello?"

"Hi, Megan, this is Paul. How are you doing today?"

"Fine, thank you." But Megan wondered why Eller was calling.

Gil, rope in hand, pulled the pig over to his truck, and as they approached he could hear Geronimo beginning to stir inside the trailer. Apparently, the horse wasn't pleased with the thought of having a traveling companion and the pig wasn't anxious, either, to be tied up again. Gil, ignoring all these hints of displeasure, soon had the pig safely secured and ready to travel.

Megan's dad watched and Gil felt Jim truly understood his need to handle and work with animals. But if that was true and Jim really felt this way, why was he so adamant that his own daughter not do the same type of work? It could be just a father thing and, as her dad, he figured Meagan would have a much better chance at a career and making money if she joined the world of business. Gil, however, believed that doing what a person liked and had a natural gift for far outweighed doing something strictly for fame and fortune.

Turning toward the older man, he said, "Thanks a lot, Mr. Wakefield, for catching the pig," and extended his hand which Jim reached out to shake. Gil looked toward the house, but still no sign of Megan. "Well, I guess unless there's something else you need me to do, I'll hit the road."

"No, I think that's it, but you be careful driving." And with that, Wakefield turned and walked back toward the house.

On his own, Gil climbed back into his pickup, drove down Wakefield's circular driveway and out onto the unpaved road leading to the highway. Even though he now had his pig back and all was well, he felt empty. Where was Megan? Why hadn't she come out to see him, to talk to him?

The night before, prior to the pig escaping and while they were still in the cab of the truck, they had engaged in a passionate kiss and Gil thought he had felt something special. Of course, all that stopped immediately when the trailer started rocking.

There was also her strange reaction when he mentioned his upcoming job in Little Rock. Could it be that she didn't want him to leave? Surely she understood this was his work and he needed to take these jobs? Or did she care for him so much that she didn't want him to go that far away? These questions were impossible to answer and all they did was provoke more. How did he feel about Megan? Was he attracted enough to her to turn down the job?

Suddenly, Gil had the answer and it scared him. He realized that he was in love with her. But would she leave him, too, like all the other people he'd loved throughout his life?

Chapter Eleven

It was just another Monday, but Gil was only too happy to put an end to his confusing weekend. After leaving Wakefield's ranch on Sunday morning, he had gone back to the movie's base camp where he dropped off the pig and Geronimo at the corral before going to his RV. This was to be his last week of work, on this film anyway. In a few days, he would have to remove the animals, his RV, and all other belongings. Luckily, he could still take them back to Gary's dad's ranch in Bastrop for safekeeping.

His mind wouldn't stop whirling and twirling. He'd slept poorly the night before but in spite of this felt fairly well rested and ready to tackle the day. Gil was also able to get a later start that morning since he wouldn't be on camera and didn't need to go by the costume and makeup trailers.

He still needed to check and feed the penned animals, though, and after finishing that task, saddled Geronimo. Riding over to the far pasture, he found the morning's shoot already in progress with the camera crew, at the moment, focused on Angela. She was wearing a long western-style dress, a large, hooded bonnet and was walking between rows of vines, picking grapes. According to the script's story line, it was supposed to be a rural vineyard belonging to the older man this young woman has just married. Ranch life is a lot different from what she's used to, having lived in the city all her life. But the heroine tries to prove to her new husband that she can handle it and joins in, helping with the chores. The hero, played by Wade Dillon, is a member of the farm's work crew who eventually meets and falls in love with the owner's new bride. Sure, it's a well-used story plot, but one, Gil knew, that worked well.

He was still on horseback and some distance away when suddenly Gil realized it wasn't Angela doing the grape-picking. Instead, they were filming an identically made-up substitute, Megan. This was quite a surprise since Gil had read the script and knew that even though there would be no close-ups, there were also no action or horseback scenes that required Angela's double. So why was Megan out there instead of Angela? He did have to admit, she was doing a mighty fine job.

Gil watched the shoot until Eller called out, "Cut. That's a wrap. Thank you everyone." Just then, another loud voice came from behind him. Turning, Gil saw that Angela's car had arrived and the fully costumed actress, yelling and screaming, emerged and, with everyone's full attention, was walking over to the set.

"Just what do you think you're doing?" she demanded of Eller.

"Why, finishing up the movie, of course," he answered calmly.

"Without me?" she asked arrogantly. Though no one thought it possible, Angela's voice was becoming even louder.

"Maybe I'm mistaken," said Eller in a cool, professional manner, "but didn't you tell me on Friday that you quit?" This drew gasps from everyone watching the drama unfold.

"Why, I never said such a thing!" yelled Angela, who, in spite of all the layers of makeup, was turning red.

"Yes. I'm afraid you did, my dear. So, since I have a movie to finish, I've asked your double to fill in and Megan's doing a beautiful job." With this, Eller turned his back on the angry star and calmly walked over to speak to a cameraman.

Left standing there alone, Angela didn't seem to know what to do or how to make a graceful exit. Finally, she marched over and got back into the car which then turned around and drove off.

Gil saw Megan, now dismissed by Eller, heading quickly in the opposite direction, probably trying to avoid any confrontation with Angela. As for himself, he didn't know where to go or what to do until Eller called out his name and put him to work, keeping him busy for the rest of the morning.

His job was moving the cows around, first here and then over there; sometimes walking and, at other times, running. Three other wranglers helped, but he was the one responsible for seeing that it was done correctly. Most of the earlier onlookers found this boring and disappeared. And he didn't see Megan anymore that morning either though he was hoping he would run into her at the catering tent during lunch break.

That didn't happen. Instead, Angela appeared just as he was about to go in and, grabbing his arm, led him over to the counter where they selected what they wanted to eat. Then it was only natural they'd sit at the same table which was okay with him as, so far, there'd been no sign of Megan.

At first, Gil was a little tongue-tied and embarrassed about having witnessed what happened earlier on the set between Angela and Eller. But she didn't bring it up and, of course, Gil didn't either. Instead they talked about, of all things, the weather. Even though there had been little or no rain to interrupt filming during these past months, Angela rambled on and on about how happy she would be to get back to sunny California. Gil merely nodded his head in agreement. Why argue over such a senseless topic? Then she asked if he had heard about a mule being let out of the pen that morning and escaping.

"A mule?" he asked. "I wonder if it was mine. Do you know if anyone caught it?"

"Yes, I think they got it back but it was quite a struggle for a while. They said a girl had turned it loose, someone who was dressed like me." Angela stopped speaking and looked directly at Gil. "But, of course, it wasn't me. Why would I do that? What purpose would it serve?"

"Well, I don't know why anyone would do it."

"Unless, of course," said the star coyly, "it was Megan. She's jealous of our relationship, you know?" Angela looked across the table and gave him a seductive smile, one that suggested many things.

Gil was becoming more uncomfortable by the minute. He couldn't honestly believe that Megan would do such a thing. Was she that mad at him and, if so, why? "What relationship are you talking about, Angela? You and I are just business acquaintances and Megan knows that. And she's a professional and certainly wouldn't turn an animal loose."

Gil, having finished his sandwich, made an excuse to leave and, in spite of the hurt look on Angela's face, hurried from the tent. Once outside, he ran to the corral and the first thing he saw was his mule, standing over by the far side of the pen chewing on a large bale of hay.

Geronimo, spotting Gil, immediately ran up to the corral railing, anticipating a nose pat and sugar cubes. The horse wasn't disappointed and the two stayed there for several minutes enjoying each other's company until Gil decided to go over to the storage building adjacent to the corral. He knew he needed to begin packing up his personal belongings and move them out of there since his part in the picture was almost finished.

As he approached, however, he thought he heard voices coming from inside the building. *Who can that be?* The door was slightly ajar and Gil heard Wade Dillon speaking to someone else. "I just don't believe Gil did that," the actor said. "Why would he want to turn his own mule loose?"

This stopped Gil in his tracks. *What are they talking about?* Remaining outside and quiet, he heard Eller reply, "Because if it got lost then maybe he could sue me and the movie company. Also, because he may have heard that I plan to fire him today."

"What?" said Dillon, echoing Gil's thoughts. "Fire him? Why in the world would you want to do that? Besides, this is his last week, isn't it?"

Eller coughed slightly and after a brief hesitation, replied, "Well, yes, but for the rest of the animal shots, I'll just call on Megan to help. She's quite good with livestock and much more dependable. And, as I said before, I'm sure he's the one who let that mule out."

"But he's the head wrangler. You can't fire him. Besides, wasn't he with you on the set all morning?" Dillon sounded confused.

"So? He just had someone else turn the mule loose. But enough of this, Wade. Let's go back to the Honey Wagon now and get cleaned up."

Gil made a mad dash to the other side of the trailer, arriving just as the two men came out.

Waiting until he was sure they were gone, Gil finally went inside. Instead of gathering up his things, Gil just stood there, unable to get the conversation he'd overheard out of his mind.

Why does Eller dislike me so much? Hadn't he done a good job on this movie? He was always on time and faithfully read the script beforehand. He knew what was expected and had provided all the right animals, so why all this? Gil, recalling Eller's strange looks and attitude whenever the director saw him talking to or standing near Angela, suddenly knew exactly what the problem was. Or, at least, he thought he did. Eller was jealous and Gil almost laughed. Poor Paul! Really, he had nothing to worry about. Gil had absolutely no interest in Angela, at least not that way.

Regardless, Eller was in a position to ruin him, his reputation and his career. And, true or not, if the director spread the word that Gil had intentionally let the mule go and then expressed his fabricated reason for Gil doing so, in order to sue him, it could very well ruin any future work Gil might have in the film industry.

But who could have let the mule out? It's hard to believe that Megan did it, but someone did see a person around there that looked like Angela. So, who else, other than Megan, could it be? Who else could have been out there this morning, wearing the very same wardrobe and makeup as Angela? These were definitely not thoughts that Gil wanted to be having about a person he now believed he loved.

"That was great spaghetti, Mom." Megan carried her plate over to the kitchen sink, rinsed it off, and placed it in the dishwasher. Since her parents had finished their lunch earlier, she had eaten alone. In fact, before she arrived, Jim had already gone to the pasture to see if any hay remained from the bales he took out there several days before. They really needed rain so that more grass and the winter hay crop could grow.

Needing to get rid of the heavy layers of makeup she was still wearing, Megan went to take a quick shower. This done, she dried herself off, put on a clean pair of jeans, a knit top, and boots. She blow-dried her recently cut, spiked hair and when finished, was pleased with the mirrored reflection.

Megan was also thankful that she wouldn't have to experience another ordeal like the one she had witnessed that morning. While Angela had been yelling and screaming at Eller, Megan felt the hateful feelings expressed were being directed at her. Could the woman actually be jealous of the attention Eller was giving her? If so, his plan was working.

And, while all this had been going on, Megan spotted Gil standing off to the side. Apparently, he arrived about the same time as Angela because Megan, in spite of herself, had been checking the area all morning just to get a glimpse of Gil. But he hadn't been there. Her feelings for this man were so mixed. In some ways Megan was glad the movie was almost over, that he would be gone, and she could get on with her life. In all honesty, though, she wanted him in her world permanently.

Fed, clean, and ready to roll, Megan, after giving her mother a quick peck on the cheek, went out to saddle her horse and found her dad in the barn.

"Hi. Mom said you were out checking cows. Is everything okay?"

"Seems to be, but they only have enough hay for today, so tomorrow I'll have to haul more bales from the barn out to the pasture. Will you be able to help?"

"I think so, Dad. And, by the way, I mailed off my resume today to Anderson Enterprises. They manufacture a variety of high-powered cleaning products and are looking for technical help in their production department. They're forming a special group to research people's needs and wants and that's the job I applied for." *But not what I want to do,* she added silently.

"Oh, that sounds great, Megan. Let's hope it works out and that you hear something soon. Any plans for the rest of the day?"

"Yeah, I have to go back to base camp. Eller stopped me just as I was leaving to come home for lunch and said he needed to talk." Picking up her saddle, Megan started to leave the barn.

"Well, tell him that I got my check, but it was only

for two weeks. Ask him if they can get the balance sent to me right away."

"Sure, Dad, I'll do that. I should be getting a check soon, too, for my work as an extra. Probably won't be as big as yours, but I'll be happy to help with household expenses." Megan left the barn and saddled her horse. When finished she said, "See you this evening," to her dad, who had followed her outside, and then she rode off.

Going through the woods that afternoon at a slow pace, Megan found it relaxing. Times like these made her realize just how much she loved the ranch; how she wanted to spend her life outdoors instead of sitting behind a desk in some stuffy office building, eight hours a day.

But when reaching the edge of the movie camp, everything changed. Life no longer seemed peaceful. This wasn't due, so much, to the activity taking place there—people hurrying from one tent, trailer, or location to another—it was more the feeling of stress and tension that seemed to fill the air. This intensified after she put her horse in the corral and walked over to Eller, who was standing in front of the catering tent. He was talking to a man she didn't recognize. She couldn't hear what they were saying, but from their body language, the subject seemed intense. However, when Eller spotted her approaching, he quickly held up his hand to the man as if silencing him, and then walked rapidly over to meet her, his face now wearing the well-rehearsed, charming smile.

"Oh, thanks, Megan, for coming. I don't have much time, so I'll make this short. Do you think you could fill in again for Angela on the set tomorrow?"

"Why, is she ill?" Megan was confused. The actress, though angry that morning, had looked perfectly healthy.

"No. She isn't sick. But because of matters I don't wish to go into right now, I need for you to do this. Can you be on the set, dressed and ready to go by eight tomorrow?"

"I guess so, Paul. What's the scene, another one in the vineyard?"

"No. In this one you'll be with Wade Dillon. Of course, there won't be any close-ups of you. If need be, we'll show Wade's face and just the back of your head." Eller stopped talking and stared off into space, lost in thought. Apparently reaching a decision, he said, "Okay this will work. Be on the set, ready to go by eight and we should have a wrap no later than noon." Eller reached out to shake Megan's hand. Then, as if suddenly remembering, he asked, "Say, since you're here, can you come over to the pen and look at a mule's leg?"

"You mean Gil's mule?"

"Yes, the one that was let out of its pen this morning."

"What do you mean, let out of its pen?" Megan was beginning to feel that more was going on here than she was aware of.

"Someone turned the mule loose. Luckily, we were

able to catch it before anything serious happened. But the animal's leg has a cut on it and that's what I want you to check out."

"But why don't you have Gil look at it?" Megan realized this issue was becoming more confusing by the minute.

"I can't do that right now, so I'm asking you. Will you look at the mule?" Eller's charismatic smile was gone and his attitude was becoming testy.

"Okay. I'll take a look."

"Thank you," said the director as Megan followed him over to the corral.

The mule was alone in a back pen and, to get there, Megan and Eller had to walk along the far side of the large corral, where the horses were being kept. Eller opened the gate and Megan followed him in. But none of this seemed to bother the animals. Even as they approached, the mule didn't seem to be nervous.

So, while the director held onto the harness, keeping the animal steady and in place, the girl lifted its rear leg for a closer look. "Yes, I see a cut here but it doesn't look bad. If you have some alcohol, I'll clean it and tape it closed. It should heal within a week but there'll be a scar."

"Well, I don't think a scar will be a problem or hurt its career, do you?" Eller asked, as both laughed at his feeble attempt at humor.

Cleaning and taping the cut didn't take long and Megan was just finishing when Gil arrived, seated astride Geronimo. He dismounted outside the mule's pen.

"What are you doing to my mule, Megan?" he asked angrily.

"Oh, hi Gil. Paul asked me to look at its leg. I found a cut, but it isn't bad. I've taped it and it should heal quickly." Suddenly, Megan felt embarrassed, especially when she saw the look that the mule's owner was giving her.

"How did that happen? When did it get cut?" Gil now appeared confused as well as angry.

"It probably happened when you let it out of the pen this morning," Eller said. Letting go of the animal, he walked over to the fence and looked directly at Gil, who was standing on the other side.

"When I let it out?" Gil shouted and Megan could see that his anger was growing. "I wasn't even here, Paul. You know I was working on the set. And besides, I heard that someone saw a girl do it, someone who was dressed like Angela." Now he glared across at Megan, still there beside his mule.

"You think it was me?" she asked. "I was on the set, too, remember?"

Eller cut in. "Well, no matter who let it out, the animal got hurt. But thanks to Megan it'll be okay in a few days." Turning to face her, he added, "I've got to go now, but we'll see you tomorrow morning, right?"

"Yes, Paul, I'll be here." Megan watched the man leave the pen and disappear behind one of the parked RVs. Turning to Gil, who was still standing on the other side of the fence, she said, in a polite voice, "I didn't mean to invade your turf, Gil. Paul asked me to look at the animal and I didn't think it would be a problem."

"Lady, you seem to be invading a lot of turf lately." With that, he led his horse over to the supply trailer and began to remove the saddle.

"What do you mean?" she asked, following him.

"Well, it sounds as if you want to get me fired so you can take over my job."

"That isn't true and you know it. You weren't here and Paul just wanted someone to look at the mule. And how dare you accuse me of letting that animal loose this morning."

"I wasn't accusing you of anything. I just stated what someone else saw. You can draw your own conclusions."

Megan couldn't believe he was saying this. How could she have been so wrong about this man? So, before losing her temper and saying or doing something irrational, she ran over to her horse. After mounting, she walked the animal quickly to the edge of the camp. There, Megan dug in her heels, causing the horse to gallop off to the woods and her house. It wasn't until she was halfway home did she realize she'd forgotten to ask Eller about her dad's check.

Chapter Twelve

It was still dark the following morning when Megan got out of bed. Selecting another clean pair of jeans, a T-shirt, and the necessary undergarments, she dressed and went to see if her mother was up yet and maybe even had some breakfast prepared. It was her lucky day.

Naomi was not only up, but in the process of frying sausage. She also offered to fix her daughter an egg, which was eagerly accepted. Sometimes Megan wondered why her mother had never pursued a career instead of settling for housekeeping and ranch work. Sure, her mom, now forty-five years old, was from a different and older generation but she knew Naomi had several strong talents, one of which was sketching. Her daughter never could understand why her mom hadn't used this to pursue a career in art instead of spending her days washing dishes, cleaning house, gardening, and chasing cows.

However, these thoughts weren't the ones circling Megan's mind at the moment. Instead, she was wondering about her own career. Should she do what she really wanted to do, look for work involving animals, especially in the movies, or follow her dad's wishes and sit behind a desk in some office?

But before she could come up with an answer her dad came into the kitchen followed by a hungry Bubba and he had good news to share. "Hi, kiddo, guess what? I received another check from the movie company and we're finally up to date."

"That's great, Dad. I know you needed the money." Megan was relieved, especially since she had forgotten to mention the missing check to Eller the day before.

"Of course, there won't be too many more checks coming. But a lot of the calves are big enough to sell now and we should be back on track, financially, for a while."

"I think this is the last week of filming." Megan had her own personal feelings about this but didn't share them with her dad. Actually, at the moment, she didn't know if she would be happy or sad to see the movie people leave; maybe a little of both.

"But," Jim went on, "it'll probably take them another week to move everything out and clean up the pasture, something they agreed to do in the contract. And I'm sure I'll be entitled to a check for that time as well."

"Yeah, if you ever get it," Naomi interjected, still standing at the stove.

"Oh, I'll get it all right. Hopefully, it won't take forever," was Jim's retort. Megan noticed, though, her dad was still smiling.

The rest of their conversation centered on ranch work, and rounding up and selecting calves for the livestock sale that week. Jim figured the film crew would be off his land in plenty of time for him to plant a hay crop before it got too cold.

Finally, her breakfast finished, Megan went off to brush her teeth. That done, and after a quick good-bye to her folks, Megan hurried out to the corral and saddled up.

It was a bit cool that morning riding through the woods, but the weatherman on TV had promised a bright, sunny day, in the seventies, with little or no wind. While, of course, this was good news for the movie company, she knew it wasn't for her dad, who really wanted some rain.

At the camp, Megan was surprised to find Geronimo grazing quietly on a fresh bale of hay in the corral. That meant Gil must be close by. So, while opening the gate and putting her horse inside, she checked out the few people she could see but there was no sign of him. *That's okay,* she lied to herself. *I didn't want to run into him anyway.*

It took over an hour to get attired in her costume and have makeup applied. She was pleased, though, that there were no long lines and she didn't have to wait at either trailer. Since the movie was wrapping up and filming was almost finished, quite a few people had already moved out and left for their respective homes. Consequently, all of her needs that morning were taken care of promptly. In fact, she noticed that a number of the previously parked RVs had been moved out. This world of fantasy was quickly coming to an end.

Retrieving her horse from the corral, she saw that Geronimo was gone and figured Gil had already come by to get him. *Maybe he'll be on the set and I'll see him when we start filming*. But that didn't make much sense either, since she had understood Eller to say that today's shoot wouldn't require any cattle. And, sure enough, when reaching the set, she saw no sign of Gil or his horse.

Stop it! her mind yelled. *Don't you know by now that where he is and what he does is none of your concern?* Somehow, though, she couldn't convince her heart.

It had been two days since Eller had assigned Gil any stunt work or asked him to double for Wade Dillon. Nor had he been told to handle any of the livestock being filmed. However, he still needed to feed and take care of the animals when they were off camera and so, that morning, before going over to the tent for breakfast, he did just that.

But, afterward, while sitting there dawdling over his second cup of coffee, he looked up and saw a familiar face coming his way. He recalled that it was the girl he had seen several days earlier having lunch with Megan and, though not sure, thought her name was Tracy something.

Reaching his table she stopped, and to Gil's surprise set her tray down. "Do you mind if I join you? I hate eating alone."

Not knowing what to say, he nodded his head.

"You do remember me, don't you?" she asked, after getting settled in her chair. "My name's Tracy Meeks. We met the other day when I was having lunch with Megan."

"Yes, of course I do. How are you doing, Tracy?" Poor Gil didn't know what to say and was groping for words.

"Oh, I'm fine. I know the movie's about to wrap up, and even though I don't have anything more to do here, I've been hanging out for the past few days, hoping to get hooked up with another shoot that might be starting soon somewhere around here. Staying in touch and talking to the right people, I've found, is the best way to pick up new jobs. Then yesterday I met a guy who works in props and he called me last night to say that he had a lead on a possible job. I'm supposed to meet him here in an hour."

"That sounds promising, Tracy. I hope it works out for you."

"Me, too, but you know this movie business, Gil. It's never a sure thing until the very last minute, and sometimes not even then."

Gil smiled. What she said was the truth. And, having finished his coffee, but not knowing how to politely get up and leave, Gil just leaned back in his chair.

"You're a wrangler, right?" Tracy asked.

"Yes I am and I also double and do stunt work."

"And you take care of those animals out there in the pens?"

Gil was beginning to wonder why she was asking these questions. Was she trying to get information from him about a movie job she could apply for?

"Yes, Tracy, I do. In fact, quite a few of them are mine. Why, do you like animals?"

"Well, sort of. But, I grew up in San Antonio. So, other than having a dog, I've never been around livestock much. It's just that yesterday morning I happened to be out near the corral and saw Angela there, letting a mule loose. It didn't want to go at first and I saw her stick its leg with something sharp like a knife to make it run out of the gate. I thought it was all very weird."

"You actually saw this?"

"Yes, I was walking up to the other side of the corral at the time."

"Are you sure it was Angela?"

"Well, I think so. She was wearing her costume, you know, the same dress and hat that I've seen her wear before on the set." Now the girl was looking at him strangely.

"Did you see her face?" Gil really hoped she had and that Tracy's answer to this could clarify the whole matter.

"Yes I did. Of course, she was some distance away and the hat was flopping over and covering it some, but I would swear it was her." Tracy sat there for a moment, thinking, and then a strange look crossed her face. "I wasn't aware of it at the time, but now thinking back, all her movements and mannerisms were just like Angela's. I've seen quite a few of her movies and I recognized that gesture she often does, you know, putting one hand on her hip and waving the other in the air? Well, she did this once or twice while trying to get the mule to move."

Gil knew immediately what Tracy was referring to. He could recall watching the actress using that mannerism both on camera and off when she was agitated, insistent, or acting that way for a part.

"Thanks Tracy. You don't know what a help you've been."

"I'm not getting her into any trouble, am I?" Tracy looked worried.

"No. This has just helped to clear up a few things. She's not in trouble, and even if she was, you certainly wouldn't be involved. I promise your name will never come up."

While Gil could see that Tracy was not entirely convinced, he let the subject drop and asked her what other films she'd appeared in. Tracy seemed happy to answer this question. And, ten minutes later, after wishing each other well, both left the tent, going their separate ways.

* * *

Megan, at first, was uncomfortable working so close to such a famous actor like Wade Dillon. In his mid-thirties, the man had already starred in enough movies to become a household name. But he was very charming and, before long, had her feeling right at home there on the set.

The night before, she had carefully gone over the script Eller had given her so she knew what to expect. For the most part, it would be close-ups of Dillon. She was being used merely as a prop and spoke no lines. First, they were filmed walking down a country road together, their backs to the camera. Then, there was the scene where they sat in chairs across from one another. The camera was facing him while he held her hands and spouted terms of endearment. Only the back of her head was visible. The final shot was done out on the street of the fabricated town. There, Dillon helped her into a waiting horse-drawn buggy and waved sadly as she was driven out of sight. Before each scene they had to change costumes, making it all take longer and using up more minutes. So, though her participation was limited, she was still getting paid for her time and found it all to be profitable as well as exciting.

Eller finally called it a wrap and that's when Megan first saw Angela. She was standing at the edge of the set. This was quite a surprise because the star never watched others act or perform unless absolutely necessary. Megan, while trying to figure out how to get off the set without coming anywhere close to Angela, then saw Wade walk over to the actress. Reaching out, he took Angela's arm and led her off in another direction. So, not wasting time, Megan ran over to the portable van, used when changing costumes, and got into her own clothes. Then, after walking her horse off the set, got up into the saddle and before long, was traveling at a fast gallop, straight across the pasture. For the first time that day, Megan felt free of all her stress.

But, this didn't last long. Soon troublesome thoughts began going through her mind and she slowed the horse down to a walk so she could think. However, this didn't work, either. And not being in a mood to deal with other people right then, Megan pulled sharply on the reins, turned her horse around and headed down toward the riverbank and solitude. Many times, while growing up, she had done this, especially when she wanted to get away from the real world and needed a place to go, somewhere to sort things out. The last time at the river, though, Megan had chased a mindless cow into the water and Gil had to rescue her.

Now there are no cows and I'll have the entire place to myself. But, as she broke through the trees and reached the riverbank, who should she find? None other than Gil! He was skipping stones across the water as Geronimo stood quietly beside him.

Gil must have heard something because, turning, he appeared stunned to find Megan there. But he wasn't as shocked as she was. Megan considered this area to be her own private retreat.

"What are you doing here?" he asked.

"I might ask you the same question, since this is my family's ranch." Megan's emotions were becoming more mixed by the moment. She really didn't know how she felt. Part of her was angry, but another part was thrilled and happy at seeing Gil.

Picking up another stone, he tossed it across the water. "I'm sorry. I know this section of the ranch isn't included in the movie's contract, but I needed a quiet place to think. And when I remembered finding you here the other day, I realized this was just the spot I was looking for."

In spite of herself, Megan smiled. "Well, I can't fault you there. In fact, I'm here for the very same reason, to think things through. The only difference is I've been coming here, to this exact place, for my entire life."

"Why, what do you need to think about?" Gil was beginning to sound a lot friendlier than the last time they'd been together.

"Well, it's pretty private and something I don't want to talk about just yet. What did you come here to think about?"

"I'm not ready to talk about that either." This seemed to end their conversation.

She urged her horse forward and began walking slowly down the riverbank. Gil climbed onto Geronimo and followed her, keeping a slight distance between them. They walked on like this for a few minutes without any conversation, both engrossed in their own thoughts.

Then Megan pulled on the reins, bringing her horse to a halt as Gil approached and stopped beside her.

"Well," he asked. "Did you get it all figured out?"

Megan looked over at him, the hint of a grin beginning to form. "Maybe, how about you?"

"I'm not sure yet." Suddenly, they both began to laugh.

Megan found, however, that having Gil so near was also making her nervous. She thought of just galloping off but figured that would be considered rude. So, jumping down from the saddle and, while holding onto the reins, she began to walk with her horse along the sandy bank.

This didn't solve the problem, though, because Gil got off his horse, too, and came over to walk beside her. Before long he reached out and took her hand, causing her to feel angry but not at him. She was the one who didn't have the guts to pull her hand away.

I can't keep doing this. It's too painful. He doesn't want to get serious and I, on the other hand, love him too much to take all this so lightly. Megan could feel herself close to tears.

"Have you given it any more thought?"

Startled, she asked, "Given what any more thought?"

"Thursday," he answered. "Are you going to be able to help me with the animals?"

She began to laugh but this time in a nervous manner rather than a humorous one.

"What's the matter, Megan?" Gil sounded worried.

"You; you're the matter."

"Me?" She could tell this wasn't the answer he had expected. It really wasn't the one she had planned to give him. The truth had simply popped out. Trying to cover it up, she groped for the first excuse she could come up with.

"I'm sorry, Gil. What I meant to say is that the problem is animals, and by that, I'm referring to my life." Now he really looked confused. So she tried again.

"I think I might have mentioned before that my dad wants me to use my degree in business to work for some big company and make lots of money. I, on the other hand, want to work with animals. So, just now, as we walked along the river here, I sorted all this out and have come to a decision. I'm going to find a way to make a living and support myself in a job that deals with animals. The problem will be trying to explain this to my dad. He's going to ask just how I plan to do this and I haven't figured that one out yet."

"What about becoming a veterinary assistant?"

"I've seriously thought about that and it's on the list. I've also been watching what you do, providing the temporary use of livestock for movies, commercials, and other events and that also interests me."

"Well, does this mean you're coming Thursday to assist me? It might help you with your decision."

Nodding, Megan answered quietly, "Okay, then. I'll come Thursday and do all that I can to help."

She was surprised that her answer seemed to please Gil. Did he like her that much and was using this as an excuse to have her near him on Thursday or was he just desperate for her assistance? Well, it didn't matter, because this was something she wanted to do. She admitted to herself, she wasn't doing this just for the opportunity to work with animals. Her reasons were much more complex than that.

By this time, Gil couldn't hold back his feelings any longer. Megan's voice, low and slightly husky, had rippled through him, stirring his blood. Reaching out, he pulled her close, tilted her face toward his and began kissing her.

At first Megan seemed to struggle as if trying to free herself from his grasp. That quickly stopped and she pressed her mouth even harder against his. Finally, coming up for air, Gil pulled his lips a short distance away and, looking down, was drawn by something almost desperate in her eyes; a vulnerability and hunger that reached out, demanding his attention. He had never before felt such a strong attraction to any woman.

Megan moved back a little, her expression serious. "Gil, I want you to know that I didn't turn your mule loose. You've got to believe me."

For a second he had no idea what she was talking about. Then he remembered what had happened the day before. "I do believe you, Megan. But you're not the only one who's been accused. Remember yesterday? Eller said that I was the one who did it. But of course that's ridiculous. Why would I do such a thing? What would be the point?"

"Well, apparently you thought I would." Megan was becoming upset and began to pull away from his arms. "How could you possibly think such a thing about me?"

Gil, on the defensive, answered, "I don't know. But after you tried to take over my job as head wrangler, what was I supposed to think?" Both were standing there, almost eye to eye and neither was contemplating a kiss.

"I did what?" Megan's voice was no longer soft or husky. Now she was almost shouting.

"I heard Eller say that he was going to fire me and give my job to you."

"Yes, I heard that, too, but he never talked to me about it. I do hope you know that I never would have accepted it."

Gil felt thoroughly confused as the two stood there glaring at one another. He didn't know what to think. Though part of him wanted to reach out and pull her back into his arms, another part said, "No." He was finding it more and more difficult to carry on a civil conversation with this woman, although he really did like her. Like her? No, he loved her!

This thought was so unplanned it caused him to take a full step backwards, as if trying to get away from the source of all his confusion. However, in doing so, he backed into the side of Geronimo, startling the horse and causing it to rear up on hind legs. In turn, this spooked Megan's horse. It began to run down the river bank, dragging Megan, who was holding on to the reins.

Gil, able to calm Geronimo right away, jumped up into the saddle and before long reached Megan and her runaway horse. She had managed to slow the animal down enough for Gil to reach out, grab the halter, and quickly bring it to a stop.

By now, a breathless Megan was covered with dirt, from being dragged along the riverbank. Getting to her feet, she tried brushing as much of it off her clothes as possible.

"Thanks for catching us," she muttered.

"No problem. Are you all right?"

"Yes, I think so." Making one final swipe at her pants, Megan put her foot in the stirrup and got up on her horse. "I guess I'd better head on home." This was said without eye contact.

"Yeah, me too," Gil mumbled as he turned his horse, preparing to leave. "Ah, are we still on for Thursday?"

A second or two passed and there was no answer from Megan. Then, while digging in her heels to prompt the horse, she said, "Yeah, I guess so," and quickly took off toward the woods.

Gil didn't move. He and Geronimo stayed put until Megan was completely out of sight before heading slowly down the riverbank, again trying to think. All he could concentrate on right then was Megan. He tried to sort out exactly how he felt about her and, of course, kept coming up with the same answer. He loved her. *So why do I keep acting like such a fool? Why do I keep letting her leave me or keep leaving her?* For this, he had no answer.

Megan arrived back at the house late that afternoon, still stressed from her earlier encounter with Gil at the river. Luckily, her parents weren't home and she was able to go straight to her room and strip off her wet, grubby clothing without having to come up with any explanation.

The long, warm shower relaxed her and before long most of the tension was gone. After dressing and blow-drying her hair, she found her parents in the kitchen, unloading groceries they'd bought in town.

"Well, how did your day go?" Jim asked right away.

Megan responded with a casual answer.

Jim inquired if she'd heard anything yet on her job applications.

"No, Daddy, but no news is good news, right?"

He didn't answer but merely stood there, staring at her. Naomi quickly stepped in and asked Megan for some help getting dinner ready, ending the conversation.

Always the good cook, Naomi outdid herself that evening with help from Megan. Within an hour, delicious smells of her mom's famous homemade lasagna were coming from the oven, a meal Megan truly loved.

It didn't take long for the three to devour their first helping, either. They went back for seconds, keeping the conversation limited to just comments on the meal.

However, as they ate their dessert of ice cream and homemade brownies, Jim looked over and asked his daughter again how her day had gone.

Taking a deep breath, Megan said, "My day went real well on the set. I filled in and was Angela's double while they filmed shots of Wade Dillon. And there were no complications." She didn't mention the incident at the river. Instead, she told them about her new plan.

"I've decided not to apply for any more office jobs. Instead, I want to work with animals. I just don't have any answers yet as to how or where, but I'll figure that out soon enough."

Megan almost giggled at the look of amazement on both parents' faces, though neither said anything for several seconds.

"What?" her dad finally exclaimed. "You're going to do what?"

"Daddy, please don't be angry. Growing up on this ranch, I have been around animals all my life. I enjoy working with them, even doing the hard stuff. And, after taking those veterinary science courses in college, my interest increased. So please don't be angry. Don't be disappointed either. I really need your support."

Jim didn't say anything. Instead, he got up from the table and left the room. Naomi, however, reached over and patted her daughter's arm. "It'll be fine. He just needs some time."

Chapter Thirteen

"Well, folks, after we finish shooting today, this movie will be a wrap." Paul Eller had asked everyone connected with the picture and who was still in the area to meet on the main street of the western town set at eight o'clock that Wednesday morning. He'd even called Megan the night before to make sure she would be there. She was scheduled, afterward, to go before the camera for several more shots needed to connect some previous scenes done by Angela.

The director spouted his usual dialogue, the same one given at the completion of each of his movies; thanking all for their tremendous help and telling them to be sure to turn in their vouchers, time cards, and invoices so that final checks could be sent out. Then he extended an optimistic wish that they all could work together again, soon.

Throughout all this, Megan noticed that many of those listening appeared bored. However, since all this was new to Megan, she hung onto his every word. But when he mentioned the wrap party that evening at Toby's Restaurant in Wayside, most of the onlookers perked up and some halfhearted but enthusiastic cheers arose.

Eller finished speaking, finally, and the expected response of mild applause came from the group as those not involved in the day's shoot began to leave. Megan, standing out of the way, saw Gil and Angela on the other side of the set's main street. They seemed to be having a serious conversation and Gil kept raising his hands, as if trying to pacify the actress. Unable to restrain herself, and since most of the crowd had dispersed, Megan stepped further back into the shadows of the nearest fabricated building so that she could continue to watch this unfolding drama unobserved.

Angela was growing more agitated. The volume of her voice had amplified and though Megan couldn't hear the exact words she could detect from her tone that she was angry and upset; and using the trademark Angela was known so well for, one hand on her hip and waving and pointing the other. Finally, in a huff, the woman turned and marched over to her chauffeured car. *Now, that's strange,* Megan thought, leaving the shadows and hurrying over to Eller.

At first, she thought the director was talking to a member of the camera crew standing near him. But as she got closer she discovered the cameraman was talking, instead, on his cell phone and Eller, with a strange look on his face, was staring at Angela's car as it drove off the set. *Did he also see the argument between Gil and Angela?*

She had felt, for quite a while, that Eller was attracted to his star and wanted a personal relationship with Angela, something much more than just their professional one. Megan knew that she, herself, had been nothing but a pawn, used by Eller to make Angela jealous. The director must have realized this wasn't working and saw Angela had her sights set on Gil. This, in turn, had provoked Eller's antagonism toward the head wrangler. He wanted to get rid of Gil and limit any contact between him and Angela.

I'm sure relieved that this movie thing is almost over. Megan thought. *No, I'm really not glad at all,* she then admitted honestly.

"Ah, Megan," said Eller, "you're here, so I guess we'd better get started. If we do well, it should be a wrap by noon. Go get your horse and I'll meet you over there at the edge of the set." Eller appeared happier and more upbeat than Megan had ever seen him, and this time she didn't think it was an act.

The schedule for the day's filming, as explained to Megan, didn't sound difficult. First, she was to gallop down a recently made gravel path and into some wooded area. Next, she was to ride at a fast trot down the imaginary town's main street, past the saloon, while portable fans blew in the background, causing a wind storm that stirred up the sand around her. Then, for her final scene, they had her emerging from the trees to return, via the gravel path, from where she had started but this time she was to walk along slowly.

Megan began to perform these tasks, some at least twice that morning, and found she was enjoying every minute of it. Most were so simple and natural that her mind frequently drifted off to other subjects. But hearing Eller call out more directions, "Megan, turn your horse around and please repeat what you just did," caused her attention to quickly return to the present.

Methodically, she followed each of the director's commands until suddenly they stopped. Megan, still sitting atop her horse, looked over toward the director's chair and found it empty. Paul Eller was gone. *Where can he be? He was right there only minutes ago.*

Turning the animal around, she began checking out the set and that's when she saw Eller talking to Angela, who must have returned while Megan was acting. At the exact moment she saw him, Eller looked up and saw her too. Waving his hand, he signaled Megan to approach.

Since the director was some distance away, she decided to just ride her horse over to where he stood, her biggest worry being the woman there beside him. Megan had been avoiding Angela for days and now they would be face to face.

Stopping a short distance from Eller and Angela, Megan dismounted and, holding onto her horse, walked over to where the two seemed to be having a friendly conversation. Preparing for the worst, Megan took a deep breath. "You wanted to talk to me, Paul?"

"Ah, yes, I do," said Eller who seemed happier than she had seen him in a long time. Even the actress was smiling. "Angela and I have been talking and we think that the last scene scheduled for today will go better if she does it herself. This way we can have the cameras come in closer to capture her actual facial expression and emotion. This isn't a problem for you is it, Megan?"

"No, I guess not," she said, feeling slightly put out. While she, of course, wanted to perform as much as possible, it really wasn't a big deal. Megan had already worked almost three hours and the last scene was short and wouldn't take more than half an hour at the most. "Does this mean that I'm finished and can leave?"

"Yes, you can, and thank you, Megan, for doing such a good job. We'll see you at the wrap party tonight, won't we?"

"Probably so."

Then Angela reached out and, taking Eller's arm, leaned in closer and whispered something in his ear, something that caused him to grin. Megan wondered if this sudden amicable interaction had anything to do with the star's earlier strained conversation with Gil. Well, whatever the reason, there was no doubt in Megan's mind that Eller was enjoying and savoring every moment.

Turning to leave, Megan suddenly realized this

would probably be the last time she'd ever see this fabricated western town. By the end of the day, all the filming would be completed and the set, no longer needed, would be dismantled. So, slowing her horse down even more, she took this final opportunity to look around.

It wasn't just a set to her, anymore. Personal memories were involved as she recalled her role as a lady of the evening behind those swinging bar doors. While to some, all this might be considered nothing at all or simply just another job, for Megan she had enjoyed every moment and would love to try it again.

She doubted, however, that her dad would ever let another movie company film on his ranch. Even though it brought in the money needed, he still blamed them for his daughter's career decision. This, of course, was far from the truth. For years Megan had wanted to work with animals instead of computers. She just hadn't found the courage until now to share this information with her dad.

Gil's last day on the job started out okay, with him making it on time to Eller's eight o'clock meeting. Then things began to go sour.

It began when Angela approached him. "Hi, Gil," she had said as she reached out to adjust his collar and then left her hand resting on his shoulder. Uncomfortable, he had backed away, trying in a polite way to discourage her. However, this had just the opposite effect and Angela came on even stronger.

"You heard Eller say there will be a wrap party tonight, so how about you pick me up around seven-thirty?"

"What?" Gil was puzzled.

"Well, if seven-thirty isn't good, what time would you prefer?"

"I'm sorry, Angela, but I won't be able to take you to the wrap party." By now, all Gil wanted to do was get out of there but she wasn't through yet.

"Well, you are going, aren't you?"

"Yeah, I guess so."

"Okay, then if it isn't convenient for you to take me, how about you bring me home afterward, instead? I'm sure you'll find it worth your while. You could even come up to my suite and have a drink to celebrate the movie." Angela's hand had moved to again rest on his shoulder.

Gil, having had all the pressuring he could stand, now stopped trying to be polite. "I'm sorry, Angela, but I'm just not interested and, besides, I've made other plans."

"With whom, that mousy Megan witch?" It was apparent that Angela was enraged.

"That's really none of your business, is it?"

Still furious, Angela continued to stand there, trying to determine her next course of action. Finally, giving up, she stomped off to her waiting car. Even though all of this was confusing and uncomfortable, Gil actually felt a little flattered at having received so much attention from such a beautiful and sexy movie star. The real fact was, though, he couldn't ignore his feelings for Megan, someone who didn't seem to need or want him at all.

Leaving the set, and after returning back to the camp, Gil went directly to the shed by the corral to begin packing up his personal items. This was the easy part. Moving all the animals back to Gary's ranch in Bastrop would be more difficult and require several trips with the stock trailer. He just hoped there was no rush; that it wouldn't have to be done until after the commercial shoot the following day. During times like this, he really wished he had a partner, someone who could help him out with all these details. Too bad Gary wasn't still his cohort and could help.

Finishing up in the shed, Gil decided to check on the penned up animals. Stepping out the door to do this, he saw Megan tying up her horse.

"Hi, there," he said. "Have they finished the shoot already?"

"Not quite. Paul pulled me out and is having Angela do that last scene instead. How come you're here?"

"I'm trying to get my things together and ready to go so I'll know where it all is when I pull out."

"And when will that be?"

"Hopefully not until after we do that commercial tomorrow." Gil watched carefully for Megan's reaction to the term *we,* unsure if she still planned to help.

"Oh, they probably won't rush it. It's going to take a while to get everything dismantled and off our ranch, so having your animals and other things here for another day or two shouldn't matter. Are you going to the party tonight?"

This question, again a surprise, didn't bother him like earlier when Angela asked it. "Yes. Are you?"

"I think so. I've never been to a wrap party before, but it sounds like fun and also a nice way to say goodbye to everyone."

"Yes, it is and I think you'll enjoy yourself. Are you going with anyone?"

Megan looked at him strangely and didn't seem to know why he was asking her that. Even he didn't know why. It had just popped out.

"No."

"Well then, how about I pick you up around six and give you a lift?" Why did he feel so nervous asking her this? He had invited girls out lots of times. Was he afraid that she would say no?

But she didn't. "Oh, that would be great. Then I won't have to drive myself."

Now, neither knew what more to say so Megan began patting her horse's nose while Gil watched. Finally, he asked, "Have you had lunch yet?"

She shook her head.

"Well then, shall we go see what they've got over at the tent?"

"Okay." Megan opened the corral and led her horse inside while Gil made sure the door to the shed was closed and locked. Then, the two headed off, this time in the same direction.

Megan was ready and anxiously waiting when Gil arrived promptly at six. Earlier, she had taken a long, warm bath before putting on a rather form-fitting black silk dress, one she thought helped accent her large gray eyes. Then she arranged her short blond hair that had been modified from the spiked look her dad so strongly disapproved of, to a swept-back, more sophisticated style.

Jim and Naomi both seemed surprised when their daughter emerged from her bedroom. Megan, noticing the pleased look passing between them, hoped this meant they realized she was an adult, ready to begin her own life and make decisions for herself. Since their recent and abruptly ended conversation at the dinner table, no one, including Megan's dad, had mentioned her recent career choice.

Though expecting it, Megan jumped slightly when the doorbell rang. She couldn't understand why she was so excited and nervous. After all, she had been on dates before, if that was what this was, and had gone to plenty of parties. But when opening the front door and noticing the surprised, yet pleased expression on Gil's face—the same look her parents had exhibited earlier—Megan's nervousness instantly changed to impish amusement.

"You look terrific," Gil said with sincerity.

"Thank you, kind sir. And you don't look half bad yourself." Gil was attired in black trousers, white shirt, bolo tie, and a gray tweed jacket.

Politely acknowledging the compliment, he asked if she was ready to leave. Megan's nod prompted Gil to reach out, and gently taking her arm, they left the house and walked over to his pickup. Opening the passenger door, Gil graciously helped her inside, making Megan feel like a princess.

She continued to enjoy the relaxed, comfortable drive to Wayside and Toby's Restaurant. Just being there with Gil seemed so natural, as if this was where she was always meant to be. If only he would think of her as more than just a friend and colleague. There were moments when she thought his feelings might be growing stronger but something always came along to stop it. However, being friends was better than nothing.

They weren't the first to arrive and, pulling into Toby's parking lot, the only spot they could find was at the far end. Again, Gil walked around to help her out of the truck. And this time, instead of taking her arm, he held her hand as they entered the restaurant.

The large main room and bar was full, something that usually didn't happen on a Wednesday night, but the wrap party was responsible for most of the people there. Megan recognized quite a few of the actors she'd been in shoots with, though she would have had a hard time putting names to each one. Then a voice called out, "Hey, Gil, over here!" Bob, one of the wranglers, was standing at the bar motioning them over.

"Hi, guy," said Gil, letting go of Megan in order to shake hands with the wrangler.

"Hi, yourself," Bob said, picking up his bottle of beer. "It's about time you got here."

"Yeah, and it sure doesn't look like we're the first." Gil gazed around the room.

"Nope, I got here over an hour ago and there were already quite a few people. But I think they're just about ready to serve dinner so why don't we go into the other room where they have the tables set up. Maybe we can even get seats together." From the pink tinge to his face, Megan could tell this wasn't Bob's first beer of the evening.

As the three walked toward the private dining area, Megan saw Paul Eller and Angela at the other end of the bar. He had his arm around the star's shoulder in what looked to Megan like a sign of possession more than a show of warm emotions. Angela, however, seemed completely unaware of his arm or even the man himself. Her eyes kept circling the room, apparently keeping tabs on the various male members of the group.

Reaching the dining room, they found no one else had gone inside to sit down at any of the long tables. Larry, who Megan knew to be the owner and manager of Toby's, was standing in the doorway and personally invited them to enter. Since no seats had been assigned, they chose three at the far end of one table and, before long, other cast members claimed the remaining seats.

Each table was covered with a festive cloth and decorated with a broad, flowered centerpiece. The food was served from a pre-selected menu of roast beef, baked potato, and broccoli—simple, yet delicious. Tossed salads were served before the main course and a choice of homemade apple, blueberry, or peach pie was offered as dessert.

Megan enjoyed sharing all this with the others connected to the movie, but especially with Gil. When most of the cast and crew had finished their dessert, Eller stood up and, tapping his wine glass with a fork, tried to claim the attention of all. He wanted to make another speech.

"Well, that was a good, tasty meal, wasn't it?" he asked the group.

Everyone responded with enthusiastic applause. "First, I want to thank each and every one of you for all your tremendous help in making this picture a reality. Without you, this would have never happened. Also, a special thanks to our stars, Angela and Wade. You both did a terrific job." Megan noticed the actress, though trying to appear humble, had actually started to glow.

Eller, who loved the sound of his own voice, continued talking, though by now he had lost the attention of most of his audience. However, he rambled on a while longer before bringing his message to a close with another expression of appreciation. Eller reached out, took Angela's hand and, inviting all to join him on the dance floor, left the room.

Megan felt someone tap her on the shoulder. "May I have this dance?" Assuming this request was from Gil, her surprise was quite evident when she turned and found Bob standing behind her chair. It seemed that Gil had already gotten up unnoticed during Eller's speech, and was across the room talking to another man.

Not knowing exactly what to do, she said, "Sure, I guess so," and the two headed toward the dance floor in the restaurant's main room. Passing by Gil, who was still involved in conversation, she noticed a strange expression cross his face as he watched them leave the dining room together.

The tune on the jukebox had a fast pace to it and Bob, a good dancer, led Megan around the floor with ease. When that song ended, she declined a second dance. As they headed back to the bar where Gil was sitting, Megan suddenly felt herself being pushed aside and separated from Bob. Baffled, she found Angela edging herself in between them, grabbing Bob's arm. The star leaned in close to the young man and said, "Hey, big boy, what do you say we try out this song together?" Then, without waiting for an answer, she began pulling Bob back toward the dance floor.

Megan, her mouth gaping, watched as the star led a quite willing Bob back to the dance floor. Before long, the two were in each other's arms, swaying to the music, this time a slow piece, and Megan saw Eller's face growing more crimson by the minute. Gil, who was now standing beside her asked, "May I have this dance?"

"I'd be delighted," Megan answered. Entering his arms and becoming one with the music, Megan found it breathtaking to be, once again, this close to Gil and hoped it would last forever.

Eventually, though, the music ended. But instead of leaving Gil held onto her hand as they remained on the dance floor, waiting for the next song to begin. Although not actually in his arms, they were still only inches apart as Megan felt her emotions begin to soar. *I love this man. Oh, yes, I do love him. Now, if he would only love me back.*

Then, as if on cue, Angela showed up. "Gil, honey," she cooed, "I think it's time for our dance. You don't mind if I steal him, do you, Megan?"

Having been taught manners throughout her life, Megan knew the correct answer was, "No, of course not." But at that moment Megan wasn't feeling very polite. In fact, she was feeling anything but!

"Sorry, Angela, I do mind. Why don't you just run along now and steal someone else's partner. I'm sure you can since it's quite apparent that you've had lots of practice."

Both Gil and the movie star were speechless. Megan could see the actress' anger building and was pleased to note the smile on Gil's face. Just then, another song began and, without hesitation, Megan and Gil automatically reached out for one another and were soon gliding across the floor in time with the music. Angela, realizing that others were observing all this, donned a bogus smile, laughed at an imaginary joke that supposedly had passed between the three of them and, after a casual wave, left the floor.

As Megan watched, the actress immediately sought out Eller's company, which seemed to please him thoroughly. *Doesn't he ever get tired of the way she uses him?* Megan wondered, realizing Eller loved this woman and couldn't help himself.

I hope love never causes me to be as gullible as Eller is. At that moment, engulfed in Gil's arms, Megan wasn't able to predict anything for sure. She just snuggled closer, letting her mind drift off in time with the music.

Chapter Fourteen

As Gil pulled into the driveway, Megan saw that, except for the porch light, the house was dark. *Good,* she thought. She really didn't want to go into detail with her parents, right then, about the wrap party. There would be time enough in the morning to do that.

It had been a very pleasurable evening. Megan knew she had enjoyed herself and from Gil's manner she guessed that he had too. With no more interference from Angela they had danced the night away. Eller managed to keep close reins on the woman except when he went into the men's room and she took Bob back onto the dance floor. Megan and Gil happened to be at the bar then, having a drink, and witnessed this along with Eller's reaction when he returned. Not pleased, he had rushed onto the dance floor and, when the song ended, took Bob's place.

By this time, Megan and Gil felt they had done enough celebrating for one night so with several others they left the restaurant and headed home. Now, parked in the driveway, Megan was exactly where she wanted to be, sitting close to Gil in his truck, feeling the warmth of his body mingling with her own. It was a magnetic sensation; one that steadily drew her in.

"What time will we be leaving in the morning?" Megan asked.

"In the morning?" Gil asked quizzically. "Oh, you mean to do that commercial. Well, I guess I'll be here to pick you up around six, if that's okay."

Megan was amused by the fact that her presence seemed to be a distraction for him, enough to even cause him to forget his work. "That's fine. But I guess I'd better get inside so I'll be wide awake and able to do my best tomorrow." Even while saying this, Megan hoped he would convince her to stay a little longer.

He did. Leaning over, he brushed his lips tenderly against hers. The subtle kiss continued until she began to respond in a more passionate manner, and then it grew in pressure and insistence. Megan uttered a soft sound of pleasure and her hands found their way up around his neck as his circled her waist, pulling her nearer. She reacted to his touch and before long felt her lips molding fervently against his, causing her to whimper. She trembled as his hand ran lightly across the crown of her head.

Megan wanted this moment to go on forever. She knew she loved Gil but she feared that for him this was just another romantic end to a casual date. Then she remembered that it wasn't even a date. All he had done was offer her transportation to the wrap party.

These thoughts killed her mood. Pulling away from him, she muttered something about going inside.

"Why? What's your hurry?" Gil seemed puzzled. "I thought we had something going here."

"That's the problem. I just don't know what that something is." Megan felt she was on the verge of tears and certainly didn't want that to happen. It would be too embarrassing.

Trying to regain some form of composure, Megan removed herself from Gil's embrace while reaching for the door handle. Just her luck! She couldn't seem to find it.

"Megan!" Gil's tone was abrupt and commanding. "Stop this right now and talk to me. What's the matter?"

"I don't know."

"Yes you do. Now tell me." His voice began to sound angry. "I thought we were friends, that you liked me."

"I do like you and that's the problem." By this time Megan was feeling desperate and couldn't help or stop herself from confessing everything and telling the truth. "In fact, I think I love you." Then, burying her face in her hands in an attempt to hide her embarrassment, Megan heard his sudden intake of breath.

Clearing his throat, Gil finally found enough voice to ask, “You do?”

Megan wanted to kick herself. How could she have put them both in this horribly awkward position? Trying to rectify the moment, she said, “Yes, I do love you. But I’m not asking for anything. Maybe we can just continue to be friends and I promise I won’t ever bring this up again.” Removing her hands from her face, Megan looked over at the ruggedly handsome guy sitting beside her.

His reaction was totally unexpected. He began to laugh.

This made Megan furious, and she tried again to find the handle and open the truck’s door.

“Wait!” he called out. “I’m sorry. I didn’t mean to hurt your feelings.” But she was still wrestling with the door. So he grabbed her free arm and swung her around to face him. “I said I’m sorry,” he repeated. “It’s just that I love you, too, Megan.”

Her struggling stopped and the truck’s cab became perfectly silent. Neither spoke but rather both seemed amazed at what he had just said. Finally Megan asked, “You do?”

Moving closer, Gil gazed into her eyes and said, “Yes, I do.” He kissed her again. This time it was a sweet, simple exchange of affection and after a moment their lips parted.

"I didn't know you felt this way," Megan said.

Gil, shaking his head in amazement replied, "I didn't know you felt this way, either. I thought I was all alone."

"Me too. I wonder why we were so afraid to let each other know." This time the kiss lasted longer, was less tender, and more demanding. Megan could detect his hunger and was sure he could sense hers as well. Never having felt this way before, she found it truly incredible.

Gil pulled back a little. "We need to talk."

Surprised, Megan nodded her head. "Okay."

"I have two things to ask you. One is whether or not you'd be interested in becoming a full partner in my business? Between us, maybe we could buy some more animals, approach more people for jobs and, if necessary, even work two engagements at the same time. You could do one while I did another. But I want you to know that until we get fully established it won't be easy or pay much. But I think we can do it. Are you interested?"

"Oh, yes! I'd be happy to be your partner. Ever since I became involved in this movie and have seen what all you do, I've had the urge to try it myself. Now, with your help and guidance, it will make accomplishing this so much easier for me."

"Okay, partner, we're a team!" Reaching out, he took her hand and shook it, making the union official.

"You said there was something else you wanted to ask me?" Megan looked directly at him, her hopes high.

"Well, yeah, but it can wait. Right now I think we

should talk about tomorrow and the commercial shoot." Much to Megan's dismay, and even though she truly liked animals, for the better part of the next hour that's all Gil talked about.

Finally, he wound down and Megan checked her watch. It was almost midnight. "I guess I'd better go in now since we'll be getting an early start in the morning." But, hoping she had time for another kiss or two, Megan didn't move and just as Gil was responding to the hint, they heard a tremendous clamor coming from the direction of her parents' house.

"What was that?" Gil asked.

"I don't know." Megan sat up straight and saw a light go on in the house. From its angle, she figured someone had just gone into the kitchen. "I think I'd better go and see what that was."

Before Gil could answer, Megan was out of the truck and running to the front door, key in hand. Just as she got the door unlocked, Gil came up behind her. They entered the house quickly and headed toward the light coming from the kitchen. There, they found her mom and dad in pajamas, standing at the opened back door, looking out. Naomi was asking, "What's going on? What was that noise?"

"I think my horse just broke through the corral gate," said Jim. "Now what am I going to do?"

"Why would it do that?" asked Gil.

Startled, Jim looked behind him into the kitchen and seemed surprised to see Gil and Megan standing there.

"Oh, hi, I was so wrapped up in all this I didn't realize you had come in." Megan's dad shook his head as if to clear his mind of sleep. "I guess something got in there and spooked my horse, maybe a fox or one of those wild hogs that have been showing up here lately. Anyway, now I've got to go out there and try to find that cantankerous beast and bring it back home."

"Do you want some help?" Gil offered.

Jim seemed surprised by the offer. "I guess I could use some, but I have no idea where to begin."

Then Megan, Gil, and Jim, still in his slippers and bathrobe, headed toward the corral with Bubba following close behind. The first thing they did was check on Megan's horse, sectioned off in another area away from the trampled gate. It was still safely contained. They checked and found that the three cows in another pen appeared okay too. The only animal missing was Jim's horse.

"Do you think it headed down to the river?" Megan asked.

Her dad scratched his head. "It's anyone's guess, but I think the best thing for us to do right now is to wait until daylight. And who knows, maybe it'll find its way back home." Jim looked up and seemed to notice the frown on Megan's face. "What's the problem?"

"Well, it's just that Gil and I have to take some animals to Austin tomorrow for a commercial, and it'll probably take all day. I don't know how we can be working there, and also be here helping you."

"You can't," said her dad. "And that's all right. I'll see what I can do by myself. If I don't have any luck finding her, maybe you can help me out when you get back tomorrow." Turning to Gil he added, "You probably already know that my daughter minored in veterinary science at Texas Tech. In fact, she's planning to have a career along those lines." Megan was amazed to hear her dad saying this with such pride.

"Yes," Gil responded. "She told me that. And it's one of the reasons I've just offered her a full partnership in my business providing animals for movies and commercials. I also supply ponies, horses, and buggy rides for company picnics and other gatherings. I really think that, together, Megan and I can build this into a profitable enterprise."

Jim seemed surprised and, when he spoke, Megan noted a tone of pleasure in his voice. "Yes, she should do well and will be a big asset to your company. I don't know what I would have done without her help all these years."

This really astonished Megan. Apparently her dad had come to terms with, and was accepting of, her career decision. He even sounded like he believed she could do a good job.

The three, having done all they could, started back to the house. Then, Megan said, "Yes Dad, Gil and I were discussing all this when we heard the noise and came to see what happened. We haven't worked out any details yet but I was just thinking, maybe he and I could rent some space here at the ranch to keep the animals?"

"I don't see why not," said Jim. "I'm sure we can work something out."

Reaching the porch, and as her dad went in the house, Megan felt Gil take her arm, pulling her off to one side. "I was amazed when you asked your dad if we could board the animals here. We never discussed that."

She couldn't tell if he was pleased or upset. "Well, I just thought of it as we were talking out there. I'm sorry. I should have asked you first. If you don't want to do this, we won't."

"Oh, I want to do it, all right. In fact, I think it's a great idea. It's just that you caught me by surprise."

"Well, I promise I won't do that again; surprise you, that is. It may take me a little while to learn the ins and outs of being a partner, but with your help and patience, I know I can do this."

"I know you can too." He reached out to give her a hug. Then, tilting her face toward his, their lips came together and the kiss began to grow until Jim, from inside the house, called out Megan's name.

Breaking away from the embrace, she answered, "Yes, Dad?"

"Your mom and I are going back to bed. Are you coming in now or should I leave the door open?"

Megan didn't know how to answer so she looked at Gil. He shook his head, coaching her to tell them no.

"I'm going to walk Gil to his truck, but I'll be in shortly. I'll use the front door so you can lock up back here."

Her dad mumbled something Megan couldn't understand and she heard the door close and the lock click.

"Well, I guess I'd better get out of here," Gil said taking her hand. Together, they walked around the house and onto the front porch.

"This has been a night I won't forget," said Megan.

"Me, either; I don't just go out and get a new partner every day." Gil squeezed her hand and pulled her closer. He reached out, touching her cheek with his fingertips. "I really think your dad is pleased with the idea."

"I think so too. In fact, his reaction surprised me." Megan waited for Gil to say something more but he didn't. So, stepping away from him, she said, "Well, I guess I'd better get inside so I can be up bright and early in the morning."

"Okay. Pick you up at six." As he leaned over to give her another quick kiss, what happened next took them both by surprise. After the kiss ended and each turned to go their separate ways, Gil spun around and said, "Wait a minute, Megan."

"Yes?" She turned to Gil, standing on the top step.

Silent for a moment, he said, "I think I mentioned earlier that there were two things I wanted to ask you."

Megan's curiosity was on high alert and, walking back over to the stairs, she stood close to Gil. Surely he could see, shining from her eyes, her love for him. Why couldn't he just accept this and admit what they both knew, that their feelings for each other were honest and true, growing stronger by the minute? He had told her earlier that he loved her, so why didn't he have the courage to now say what was in his heart?

Instead, he just stood there. He seemed bewildered, as if he didn't know what to do or say at that moment. Then, he just blurted out, "Remember before, I said I had two questions? Well, one of them was to ask if you'd be my business partner. I asked, and you accepted. Now, I'm asking you to be my partner in life. What I'm trying to ask is will you marry me?"

Megan couldn't remember just how long she stood there, her mouth gaping.

"Megan, I know this is sudden, that we've only known each other a short time; but for me, it feels so right, something I've never experienced before. I'm certain, in my heart of hearts, that you're the only one I want to spend the rest of my life with."

"I know what you're saying, Gil. I've always prided myself on being level-headed, thinking situations through before acting, and never rushing into things. With you, though, it's different. It's as if we've already known each other a lifetime. So, in answer to your question . . ."

Overcome by emotion, Megan could do nothing more than nod her head up and down, vigorously.

"Is that a yes?" he asked.

And her voice returned. "Oh yes, sir, that's absolutely, a definite, yes!"

Leaning over, Gil gave her another kiss; this one lasting much longer than the last. Megan reached up, wrapping her arms around him as if to signal she wanted to hold onto him forever. Again, their lips came together and their bodies pressed close to one another. Their kiss seemed to express the yearning they felt at that moment—the need to unite completely and be one. But they had a business to run in the morning.

Megan watched as Gil made his way back to the truck, and after entering the house, she ran into her bedroom and over to the window just in time to see its taillights disappear. With a certainty she had never before experienced, Megan realized that, unlike the temporary, fictitious characters in a movie, she and Gil were destined to be the real thing forever.